For Bonnie and Bill —
I'm proud to be your sister.

A KATE LONDON MYSTERY

LITTLE SHOP OF MURDERS

SUSAN GOODWILL

WHEELER
CHIVERS

This Large Print edition is published by Wheeler Publishing, Waterville, Maine, USA and by BBC Audiobooks Ltd, Bath, England.
Wheeler Publishing, a part of Gale, Cengage Learning.
Copyright © 2008 by Susan Goodwill.
The moral right of the author has been asserted.

The text of this Large Print edition is unabridged.
Other aspects of the book may vary from the original edition.
Set in 16 pt. Plantin.
Printed on permanent paper.

LIBRARY OF CONGRESS CATALOGING-IN-PUBLICATION DATA

Goodwill, Susan, 1957–
   Little shop of murders : a Kate London mystery / by Susan Goodwill.
      p. cm. — (Wheeler Publishing large print cozy mystery)
   ISBN-13: 978-1-59722-758-2 (softcover : alk. paper)
   ISBN-10: 1-59722-758-7 (softcover : alk. paper)
   1. Bank robberies — Fiction. 2. Aunts — Fiction. 3. Nieces — Fiction. 4. Amateur theater — Fiction. 5. Michigan — Fiction. 6. Large type books. 7. Chick lit. I. Title.
   PS3607.O59226L57 2008
   813'.6—dc22
                                     2008010798

BRITISH LIBRARY CATALOGUING-IN-PUBLICATION DATA AVAILABLE

Published in 2008 in the U.S. by arrangement with Midnight Ink, an imprint of Llewellyn Publications, Woodbury, MN 55125 USA.
Published in 2008 in the U.K. by arrangement with Midnight Ink.

U.K. Hardcover: 978 1 408 41189 6 (Chivers Large Print)
U.K. Softcover: 978 1 408 41190 2 (Camden Large Print)

Printed in the United States of America
1 2 3 4 5 6 7 12 11 10 09 08

ACKNOWLEDGMENTS

Thanks to my wonderful agent Grace Morgan for her faith, encouragement, and hard work; my acquiring editor Barbara Moore for her insight, enthusiasm, and shoe savvy; and to in-house editor Connie Hill for covering my verbal and grammatical backside. Also thanks to Kevin and the rest of the staff at Midnight Ink. You've probably noticed, it's the home of the best cover art in the world.

Thanks to Gail, Jason, Lorin, Roman, and the Writers' Retreat Workshop family for support, networking, great classes, and too much fun. To Jenny Crusie and the Cherries, especially Chris Merrill and Jessica Anderson, BTCKE.

Thanks again to Laurie Tennent for an incredible photo that makes me look better than I have any right to look.

Thanks to all my beta readers, including my sister Bonnie, Debbie K., Janice C.,

Gabriella P., Pat R., Maria B., Doreen O., and of course, my wonderful little critique group, the Witches: Sharon and Michelle.

Thanks to my neighbors and my family who showed in force at signings and gave words of encouragement all along the way.

For research, I must again thank Police Chief Gary Goss of Northville, Michigan; Nancy Peska, Executive Secretary of the Community Theatre Association of Michigan; Barabara Gowans, longtime St. Dunstan's Theatre Guild member; and special thanks to the folks at the Secret Service, whose identity, as promised, will remain secret.

Any mistakes are my own silly fault — these folks all know their stuff.

And last, I must thank Bobby for keeping the faith and walking the dogs. And speaking of dogs, let's not forget Ernie, Clara-Belle, and the late Wally Huffnagle, wonderful dogs, every one. I thank them for their love and their inspiration.

ONE

"I'll bet Mercury's in retrograde, Kate." My Aunt Kitty London's stage whisper echoed through the lobby of Mudd Lake Savings Bank. "This town's crawling with crazy people and drunks."

I ran a hand through my unruly auburn curls and tried to sound calm. "The annual Sausage Festival always attracts a weird crowd," I said.

"Never do business when Mercury's in retrograde." Kitty fidgeted from one high-heeled ankle boot to the other. "That's what Roland says, and he's an excellent astrologer."

Kitty craned her neck around a beefy guy in a baseball cap and a *Flaming Sausage* jacket. I craned with her. At the counter, our teller doled twenties into the palm of a well-dressed man with a blond ponytail.

"This woman is entirely too slow," Kitty said, her voice louder this time.

The teller, whose name tag read Chiffon, frowned and arched an eyebrow in our direction. She restarted her count.

"Let's just keep a low profile until we get this money deposited."

I pressed the bag full of the town's money tighter to my side and eyed my seventy-five-year-old aunt in her faux fur vest, leather mini, and tights — her whole outfit in shades of purple God never put on a grape. Platinum curls poked out from beneath her tasseled Shriner's fez, and dangly purple star earrings reached almost to her shoulders. It'd been forty-odd years since her last movie, but she was the closest thing Mudd Lake had to a celebrity.

Low profile might be asking a lot.

"What if Fred changes his mind about our loan?" Kitty's voice went up a notch. "If the planets are out of alignment, Fred could change his mind. Should I call Roland? Maybe Psychic Buddies? I think I have them on speed dial." She dug in her fanny pack for her phone.

"Shh! Did you go off decaf again?" I whispered. I glanced around for Fred Schnebbly, the banker who held the London family's fate in his pencil-pushing hands. His office sat dark and unoccupied. "Fred said to make our deposits, then to see him and sign the papers."

Our extremely amateur theatre group, the Mudd Lake Players, had already made it through several surprising hoops — a fundraiser, a decent cast, even renting professional-grade alien plant puppets for the upcoming show.

After the loan, maybe we could jump through that last fiery ring, but it was a doozy. With a disaster-free opening night, we could wow the CracklePops Foundation and get that theatre restoration grant.

A disaster free opening night.

The planets had better be lined up like billiard balls for this thing to come off.

I scanned behind the counter for Fred and resisted my own fidgety urges. Just our teller and one other, more familiar face behind the counter: Patrice Stikowski.

Kitty zoomed in on Patrice, who was counting and stacking bills behind a "Next Window" sign.

Kitty hoisted her tote bag high. "Halloo, Patrice!" she trilled. "Be a dear and wait on us. I've got five thousand dollars from the theatre benefit. It's making me quite nervous. Plus, Kate's got all the town's cash from the Sausage Festival." She jerked a thumb at my satchel.

I gazed at the high ceiling and sighed.

11

"Is that okay?" Patrice sent a questioning look to Chiffon. "Can I open up?"

The spring sunlight glinted off Patrice's new eyebrow rings, and her hair, dyed a conservative new-bank-teller-black, made her look like a Goth version of Snow White.

"You're not to open until Rhonda gets in." Chiffon huffed and slapped a stack of twenties on the counter. "I can't imagine where that girl has gotten to."

I sent Patrice a grin. "Thanks for trying."

"We theatre people have to stick together, you know?" Stick came out "thick" around her oversized tongue stud.

Kitty reached in her bag and pulled out a rolled-up poster. She unfurled it to reveal a picture of a giant, snaggle-toothed, man-eating-alien-plant. Underneath, the words "*Little Shop of Horrors,* opening May 25th, at Mudd Lake's historic Egyptian Theatre" seemed to drip blood.

Kitty waved the poster at Chiffon. "Might we put this in the win—"

The door behind us whacked against the wall, and we all jumped. A whoosh of breezy Lake Michigan air blew past us, and a stooped, balding man in a red plaid bathrobe and floppy slippers burst into the lobby. He scuttled past us to the counter.

I guessed him to be about eighty years old.

12

I smiled and leaned toward Kitty. "Sausage Festival fallout."

The geezer slipped around the pony-tailed man at the front of our line. He swiveled toward us and shoved his hand in his bathrobe pocket. An outline of something jabbed out through the flannel.

My smile evaporated, and my heart slammed against my ribcage. A gun?

My throat tightened, and I grabbed Kitty's hand and squeezed.

"Everybody keep calm," the old man rasped. He hacked phlegm from his throat and swiveled to Chiffon. He pulled a crumpled IGA bag from his left bathrobe pocket and kept his other pocket low, below the counter. "This is a holdup."

Chiffon flicked a curtain of beaded corn-rows over her shoulder and put one fist on her hip. She shoved the grocery bag back toward the old man and wagged a very long, very fake, green and white fingernail at him. "We're too busy for this today, Walter."

The elderly man took his hand from his pocket and cupped it to his ear. "Eh?"

My heart thudded as I watched, helpless. Chiffon hadn't seen the gun, I was sure of it.

The teller leaned over and raised her voice. "Did you get a new prescription or something?"

"What the — ?" He stomped a floppy-slippered foot. "Dang it, Chiffon, of all the times to be a pain in the butt, this ain't it. Do what I say!"

"Nuh-uh. You go on home." She brushed her hand at him. "Shoo!"

He shifted his frail frame and planted his own hands on his hips. Chiffon grabbed a chocolate-frosted doughnut from a Krispy Kreme box behind the counter and chomped off a hunk. She glared at Walter while she chewed. The two spent several long seconds locked in a standoff. No one in the bank moved.

Frozen in place, I stared at the gun-shaped object sagging in Walter's bathrobe pocket. The sound of my own heart pounded in my ears.

I poked my head up to make contact with Chiffon. I tried pointing to the pocket with my eyeballs.

No response.

I jerked my head in the pocket's direction. I stretched my eyelids wide and mouthed the word "gun."

Chiffon looked over the robber's shoulder and frowned. "You got a problem, lady?"

Walter spun around, shoved his hand back in his pocket, and glared at us. I snapped my jaw shut and made my face a blank. I squeezed Kitty's bony hand tight.

"It'll be okay," Kitty whispered, her voice very quiet.

The old man looked at Kitty, then at me. He turned back to Chiffon. Out of the corner of my eye, I watched Patrice ease her hand toward the edge of the counter. I held my breath and waited.

Walter swished his pocket into view, exposing blue-and-white-striped pajama bottoms. He pointed his pocket at the scabby double rings in Patrice's newly pierced left eyebrow.

"You! Away from the alarm. You want another hole in your fool head?"

Patrice let her hand fall and swallowed hard. Chiffon's eyes grew large. The last of her doughnut dropped to the floor.

"He's got a gun? He's got a gun? He's never got a gun." She stuck her arms in the air. "Help!"

Keeping his pocket pointed at Chiffon, Walter pushed the grocery bag back across the metal counter. Mudd Lake is a small town, and I'd never noticed until now that our teller windows were wide open — no bulletproof glass.

"Give me all your twenties," he said.

Chiffon dug in her cash drawer. She

15

grabbed banded stacks of twenty-dollar bills and dropped them into the bag. "God, Walter, are you nuts?"

I hiccupped.

"Uh-oh," Kitty whispered. "Try holding your breath."

Hic.

"It doesn't help," I said.

"I know," she whispered. "How're you going to be a law enforcement official, if you get the hiccups all the time when you're scared?"

"Shhh," I said, and hiccupped again.

The man with the ponytail moved closer to Walter.

"And you," Walter spun around and shoved his gun pocket into the man's chest. "Back off!"

Walter snatched the wad of cash from the pony-tailed man's fist. The man's empty hand hung in the air for several seconds before it fell to his side.

Walter turned back to Patrice.

I wished I knew what to do. Three weeks as an auxiliary deputy, and so far I'd only done crowd control and pooper-scoop tickets.

"I want all your twenties. Every one of 'em!"

Patrice's eyebrow rings tinkled as she

yanked money from her drawer. The old man looked around nervously.

Kitty lifted her free arm and wiggled her fingers in a wave. I hiccupped and jerked her hand. I clutched my satchel and tried not to move my lips.

"Don't draw attention to us," I whispered. Too late.

The robber squinted at Kitty. He flashed a mouth full of oversized dentures in our direction and pulled his gun hand out of his pocket. He wiggled his fingers back.

Kitty smiled tentatively and batted purple eyelashes in Walter's direction. I stifled a groan. Kitty'd had seven husbands for a reason. She was a hopeless flirt.

The bandit's attention moved from Kitty to the swarthy guy in the *Flaming Sausage* jacket who stepped closer to Kitty. He put a meaty hand on her shoulder and in a thick European accent said, "Hey buddy, we want no troubles. Just do your job."

Walter squinted at him, then rammed his hand back in his pocket and whirled. He swooped his gun-pocket at Patrice. "Hurry the hell up!"

Patrice tossed her stack of bills to Chiffon, who loaded them in the paper bag and slid it across the counter. The old man snatched it and headed for the door. He stopped in front of us.

I clutched Kitty's hand, pressed the satchel to my side, and hiccupped. My heart banged like a snare drum in my ears.

"What's in those bags?" he said. He took a step forward.

Kitty jutted her chin and squeezed her tote bag to her chest. "None of your beeswax, Walter," she said.

I moved in front of her.

"You ladies got cash?" Walter wrapped bony fingers around the strap of my satchel.

My heart slammed a rhythmic message. *Do something, do something.* I thought of that gun, the people around us, Kitty right beside me. A sinking feeling took over, and I let him pull the satchel from my grasp.

He peered at Kitty. "Hey Kitty, is that the theatre money?"

"Let him have it," I whispered and hiccupped.

Kitty must have misunderstood because she stepped around me and whipped the bag in a wide arc. She walloped Walter full in the head with five thousand dollars in tens, twenties, and miscellaneous loose change.

"Aack!" Walter staggered back a step. The IGA bag and my satchel stayed under one arm and when Walter yanked his gun hand

18

out to grab for his head, a banana flew from his bathrobe pocket.

My jaw unhinged, and I stared at the floor. A banana? A *banana?*

"No!" My breath escaped in a whoosh, and I lunged.

Walter rocked backward, took another step to steady himself, and stepped on the banana. It squished out of its skin and sailed past my left ankle.

Walter leapt at Kitty and ripped her tote bag free. She pitched forward, going in like the world's most diminutive, platinum-haired quarterback on a loose ball.

A flash of Kitty with a broken hip blazed before me. I thrust out my arm and snatched a fistful of faux-bunny. Keeping a tight hold, I swiped for the three bags with my free hand. Walter jerked backward, circled around us, and setting some sort of old-fart-in-pajamas land speed record, sprinted to the exit.

I let go of Kitty, and she hotfooted it across the lobby.

The guy in the sausage jacket, the pony-tailed man, and I all bolted for the door. Kitty got there first. She stood in the door-way.

"Walter, you're a rat's patootie!" she hollered.

A flash of plaid flannel disappeared around the corner one building away.

"You know that guy?" I said, staring after it.

"You bet I do, the jackass!" Kitty said. "I'm dating him."

Two

"What?" I gaped at Kitty.

Tires screeched. We watched a late-model blue Taurus careen around the corner, its windows mirrored with sunshine — its plates caked with mud.

"You heard me." Kitty was halfway to her car, a mammoth white 1974 Eldorado convertible with red leather interior, a.k.a. the Land Yacht. "That's Walter, let's go!"

I caught up and clutched her shoulder.

"Wait! We can't leave. The police will be here any minute." I took a deep breath of the blustery Lake Michigan air and eased it out. "You're dating him?"

"Walter's a fabulous Salsa dancer, but I'm breaking up with him as soon as we get our loot back. I'm hopping mad."

Kitty shrugged me off and crossed a strip of grass to the car. She grabbed the handle on the passenger side and yanked the huge door open.

I hesitated and listened for a siren. Nothing.

"We've got to catch him," Kitty said. "He has our theatre money, and by Godfreys, we're getting it back."

"Kitty, it's too dangerous."

"You drive," she said. "When I'm upset, I get the gas and brake mixed up."

Adrenaline fizzled through my veins and my thoughts raced: Sheriff Ben Williamson had trusted me with the Sausage Festival deposit. Then there was the benefit money — with the loan, the Egyptian's ticket to respectability. I gritted my teeth and glared at the dissipating exhaust.

I moved to the driver's door and yanked it open. I slid behind the wheel. "Let's get him."

Kitty tossed me the keys. "To think I almost went Viagra shopping with that man."

My eyes squeezed shut against the image. I popped them open and shoved the key in the ignition. "You really know this guy."

"*Everybody* knows him," Kitty said. She smoothed a tuft of errant purple fur. "He's Fred Schnebbly's uncle."

I revved the engine. "He just robbed his own nephew's bank?"

Kitty just sat there steaming.

I executed a complicated five-point U-turn and tried to think like a crook. I pressed the big accelerator pedal, and we flew over the three blocks to the bypass highway.

"I bet he took that road," Kitty pointed, "but which way?"

I glanced at the signs and took a guess. "South," I said. "There's more traffic to blend in with — and more criminals."

We roared down the entrance ramp to south US-31. The highway was empty but for two semis in the distance. I jammed my foot to the floor. The tires screeched and swallowed pavement. The thin accelerator needle slid across the big white numbers until the engine jolted us into high gear around sixty or sixty-five. We whizzed past the two startled semi drivers.

"Wow!" Kitty yelled over the howling engine. "Just like Thelma and Louise!"

"They died in that car!" I hollered.

"Details." Kitty wiggled a hand at me and squinted at the highway.

Somewhere around ninety-five miles an hour I spotted the Taurus. It crested the hill a quarter mile or so in front of us. We were closing in fast.

"Is that him?" Kitty asked.

"Yep," I said. I blew the horn and flashed the lights. "Grab my phone and call Ben."

Ben Williamson, Mudd Lake's sheriff, was a person-of-interest among boyfriends — okay, so he was my only suspect.

Kitty undid her seat belt, twisted her torso, and reached over the back seat.

I shot her a look expecting to see my cell phone. Instead Kitty hoisted an odd-looking rifle into her lap. I let out a gasp and shrieked. "What the — ? What are you doing? Are you crazy? Put that thing down!"

I swatted in Kitty's direction, and we fishtailed into the next lane. Clutching the big steering wheel with both hands, I pulled us back on course. I eased off the gas, and the Taurus racked up several car lengths on us.

"You can't just shoot him!" I looked again at the gun. "Is that the paintball rifle? From the Egyptian?"

Kitty shoved the gun barrel out her window. "Don't get your panties in a pretzel, darling. I simply want to scare him so that he pulls over."

Kitty yanked off her fez and stuck her head into the howling wind. Her hair whipped around her eyes, and she pushed it out of the way.

"I played a stellar Annie Oakley, you know," she yelled over the roaring engine.

The Taurus now had six or seven car

lengths and counting.

Kitty pulled her head back in. "Kate, he's getting away! Floor it!"

"Don't fire that thing, okay?" I took a deep breath and muttered, "I'm an idiot."

Then I punched it. The fierce 70s motor howled, and we swallowed the gap to three car lengths. Then two.

A 'P' or an 'F,' the first letter of the license plate, peeped through the mud. I cut to the other lane, pulled beside Walter's car, and blew the horn. Walter's startled face appeared pressed against the rear driver's side window. I glanced at him. Had he mouthed the word "help"? I couldn't be sure. He might've been hacking phlegm.

"Uh-oh," Kitty said. She pulled the rifle back into her lap and sent her window up. "Did I just conspire to assassinate a president?"

I glanced over at the car and blinked. From the driver's seat, former U. S. President and cigar aficionado William Jefferson Clinton looked back. He didn't blink.

"That's a mask," I said.

"Phew. Scared me for a second." Kitty patted her windblown hair.

I let off the gas, and the car gained distance on us. The gap grew back to six car lengths.

"Mask or no mask," I eyed the big man behind the wheel, his whole head encased in rubber, "we don't want to mess with Bill."

THREE

Seconds later a siren wailed to life behind us. I glanced in the mirror and watched as a state trooper fell in on our tail.

"Oh, good," I said. "The cavalry."

Ahead, the Taurus accelerated sharply and disappeared over a ridge. Red flashers and blinking headlights filled my rearview mirror. The trooper jabbed his finger toward the shoulder.

"Go around!" I stuck my hand out the window and motioned for the trooper to pass me. I pointed ahead. "Up there!"

He jabbed at the shoulder again.

I waved some more and poked in the Taurus' direction.

Behind me, the trooper shook his head and kept his finger aimed at the side of the road. He mouthed the word "now."

"Crud," I muttered, and coasted to the gravel.

The trooper rolled to a stop behind me. I

hopped out of the car, my heart pounding.

"What are you doing? That's the bank robber from Mudd Lake. up ahead of us in that Taurus. You're going to lose him — them!"

"Uh-huh." The officer unsnapped his holster and tapped the butt of his gun. "Back in the car, ma'am — license, registration, proof of insurance."

I slid behind the wheel and fumbled in my purse for my license. "I don't believe this," I muttered. "I think I'm getting a ticket!"

Kitty still held the paintball gun on her lap.

The cop loomed at my window. I pressed the button and slid it down, then pointed at the highway. "That's the bank robber up there. He's getting away!"

"Ma'am, do you have any idea how fast you were going?"

He spotted the paintball rifle, and his eyes narrowed. He unsnapped his holster and rested his hand on his gun.

"Ma'am, is that a firearm?"

"It shoots paintballs," Kitty said. "We were in pursuit. Kate's in law enforcement, almost." She stuck a thumb over her shoulder. "Over in Mudd Lake."

"It's a theatre prop." I tried to smile and

send reassuring vibes. I glanced at Kitty. "It's harmless . . . Colorful, but harmless."

"My boyfriend, he's up there with Bill Clinton," Kitty said. "I'm dropping him as soon as we catch him and get the loot back. My boyfriend, not Bill."

The trooper rolled his eyes. "God, I hate that Sausage Festival." He held one hand out, the other stayed on his gun. "Hand me that thing, real slow."

"I really am an auxiliary deputy." I handed him the gun. "I'm new. For the festival."

"Uh-*huh.*" The trooper peered into the back seat. "Any other weapons? Sharp objects? Cannabis?" He wrinkled his nose and sniffed. "Have you two been to the Oom-Pah-Pah tent? Sampled the beers, maybe?"

"It's ten a.m.!" My simmering adrenaline finally boiled over. "That's the robbers! You're wasting time!"

Kitty retrieved her fez from the floor and set it atop her discombobulated hair.

"Idiot . . ." she muttered.

A vein popped into view on the trooper's forehead. He jabbed a long finger toward me. "In the back of my cruiser. Now!" He pointed at Kitty. "You — wait here, or I'll cuff you to the steering wheel."

Kitty crossed her arms across her furry

vest and glared.

Exasperating minutes passed in the back of the cop car while I recited my ABC's backward and blew into a little plastic tube. I finally convinced the trooper to call in about the robbery. Seething, I stalked back to the Eldorado.

Kitty huffed and poked her head around to peer over the back of her seat. "That man is a moron."

"He's not too happy about you and your paintball rifle, either. What were you doing with that thing, anyway?"

"I was thinking of playing one of those survivalist games out at the fairgrounds. Good exercise. Lots of men." Kitty turned to face front. "Here he comes."

The trooper motioned to the window. I slid it open, and he shoved a clipboard in my lap. I looked down at a traffic citation.

"Sign here."

"Four points!" I yanked the ticket off the clipboard and flapped it at him. "One hundred dollars . . . ? For what? For trying to be a good citizen?"

"You can pick up the paint gun at the station," the trooper said, "after the Festival."

"Twit," Kitty muttered.

The trooper's eyes narrowed again. He poked his long finger at Kitty. "I've had just about enough of you, granny."

Kitty rose off the passenger seat until her fez tassel brushed the ragtop roof. I cringed, scrawled my name across the ticket, and waited.

She ignited like a blast furnace. "Granny? *Granny?* Why, I have a good mind to report you to the Gray Panthers! The crooks are getting away with our loot while you hand out tickets with your thumb up your —"

"Woops!" I forced my sweetest smile. "Just a sec, please." I pressed the button sending the window up.

"Kitty . . ." I turned and whispered, "something's wrong. Let's not make things worse."

Kitty glared past me, then squeezed her Purple Passion lips in a tight line and nodded.

I opened my door and climbed out. The trooper eyed me, snatched the clipboard and ripped off my part of the ticket. He shoved it at me and turned on his heel. I was struck yet again by how unattractive law enforcement shoes could be.

"Officer, wait, you have my keys."

I crunched along the gravel behind the trooper as he stalked toward his car. A semi whizzed by, splattering mud on my second best-pair of boots, last season's deal of the century, black kitten-heeled Jimmy Choos.

I stared down at my glop-splattered boots. Lovely.

At the car, I took my keys from the trooper. "Sorry about my aunt. Did they catch the robber?"

He slid into the driver's seat. "You are darned lucky I don't haul you both in. There was no robbery at Mudd Lake Savings Bank. None."

I opened my mouth but no sound came out. I gazed after his taillights as he pulled away from the shoulder.

"No robbery?"

I scooted behind the wheel of the Land Yacht and put the car in gear.

"Let's go back to the bank." I told Kitty what I'd just heard from the trooper.

She stared at me. "How bizarre!"

As we pulled off the bypass Kitty produced a green rabbit's foot from her fanny pack. From it dangled a shiny brass key.

"That's the last time I let Mildred fix me up. She plays decent canasta, but her matchmaking skills are lousy."

The key glinted and winked in the sunlight.

I'd love a lead on the money before I had to face Ben and admit to being mugged with a piece of tropical fruit. "Is that Walter's?"

"You bet it is. I left a few personal things there. I want them out, pronto."

I knew we should head to the bank first or at least call Ben. "What kind of personal things?"

"Your new Stuart Weitzman boots — they're in Walter's coat closet," Kitty said.

"My Stuart Weitzmans?" The tires squealed as I made a hard left.

We drove to Wycoff Hill, a pricier neighborhood made up of older Victorian homes with an elevated view of Lake Michigan. At the foot of the hill, Kitty pointed to a careworn Victorian divided into several apartments.

Kitty reached for her door handle. "I should've stuck to younger men," she said.

"You were careful with them, right? My new boots? I mean, they were on sale and everything, half-off I think, but still . . ."

Kitty whisked a hand in my direction. "I borrowed them for the VFW dance. I wore my sneakers home. It was raining, and I know how persnickety you are about your footwear."

I followed Kitty across the ornately trimmed porch. Kitty stepped up to a door and pushed on it. It creaked open.

She glanced at me. "I guess when you're the criminal, you don't have to worry about locking doors and whatnot."

Kitty opened the coat closet and poked around. I hesitated and took in the room: a saggy, overstuffed couch and a square coffee table stacked with travel magazines — across the way, the bedroom, and beyond that a bath. At the far end of the living room, a doorway framed by shutter-like louvered doors opened to a miniscule kitchen. Walter kept a clean house for a Salsa-dancing, crazy-outlaw octogenarian.

I fought back an urge to scream. Instead, I squeaked out a hiccup, high in the back of my throat. The only thing out of place was the bloody body sprawled across the kitchen floor.

FOUR

Kitty appeared at the kitchen doorway beside me. She lifted my slouchy black Stuart Weitzmans and wiggled them.

"I finally found them under the couch." She followed my gaze. "Good Godfreys in sweat socks!"

"Kitty, dial 9-1-1, okay?" I swallowed a hiccup and took a step into the kitchen.

The body was male — face down, in a suit, not a bathrobe. A hole gaped in the back of his navy pinstriped jacket, and his pockets had been turned inside out. A pool of blood had spread across the black-and-white tile floor. I knelt beside the body and felt around the neck. Nothing. The skin felt cool.

Kitty said, "Should I do CPR? I learned it on the set of *Housewives from Outer Space*." She hugged my boots to her chest. "I had to perform it on the rubber alien. That director was a stickler for realism."

I turned to her. "I'm pretty sure . . . he's um . . ."

"Been iced?" She went gray under her Merry Mauve blush. "My heavens!"

I screwed my face up into a wince and slipped my hand under one motionless shoulder. I peered at the ashen face. It was Fred Schnebbly, the bank's CEO, Walter's nephew.

A smaller red hole with singed edges marred the front of his suit, right over his heart. That confirmed it. Fred Schnebbly was very, very dead.

A board creaked. A hulking man-shaped shadow moved across the living room wall. I froze.

I put my finger to my lips, then pointed. Kitty looked past me to the shadow, and her green eyes grew large. I helped her over Fred's body and eased the shutter-like doors closed. We were now trapped in the tiny, windowless kitchen.

With our loan officer. Our extremely dead loan officer.

I hiccupped. Like abject fear and jalapeno peppers and clowns and about a dozen other things, dead people give me the hiccups.

Don't think about it, I thought. I looked down at Fred, thought about it, and hiccupped.

From the far end of the apartment, drawers slid open and things rustled and clattered. Cupboards creaked and slammed.

Then footsteps and a voice: "Did you find it?"

"No." A deeper, more baritone voice and rustling. "He was in this place all night. It must be here."

"If we don't find it, we'll never get our promotions," the first voice said.

Now seemed like a good time for that 9-1-1 call, but I'd left my phone in the car. I pointed at Kitty's fanny pack and held my thumb and pinky to my face.

Kitty handed me her cell. The second my finger connected with the nine button, the phone gave off a loud beep.

Kitty and I both gasped.

The shuffling in the other room stopped. "Somebody's in the kitchen."

I held my breath while footsteps came toward the doors and stopped.

I tossed Kitty the phone and whispered, "Call 9-1-1."

I combed the room for something to use as a barricade — anything. The room, smaller than most walk-in closets, contained no furniture. A stove sat to the right of the doors. I tugged, but the gas line held it tight.

I pulled at the fridge. It moved, but Fred's body lay between it and the doors.

More heavy footsteps thudded toward us.

I motioned Kitty to move back, then gripped the refrigerator with both hands and yanked. The mammoth Kenmore crashed sideways to the floor. I dropped to my knees and shoved it. Fred's body flipped over like a large, stiff pancake. His sightless eyes stared at the ceiling as if to ask that universal question, *Why me?* I hiccupped and rammed my shoulder into the appliance's backside. Fred rolled sideways, and I wedged him in.

Through the slats loomed a silhouette — a very big silhouette, then both doorknobs rattled a few times. I suppressed another hiccup, and blood rushed into my ears.

Heavy breathing came from the other side.

"Get your asses out here this minute," the baritone said.

The doors rattled, and Fred's knees gave off sick popping noises.

I grabbed a frying pan and holding my breath, gripped it with both hands. I hoisted it high over my head.

"Where's Fred?" It was a new voice, more tenor in pitch.

"What is this, frickin' Grand Central?" the baritone said. "We're busy here."

"Hold it right there. Don't move."

Rustling, then Baritone Voice again, "What are you doing? Put that away!"

I knelt behind the fridge and peered through the louvers. I made out a big man in a denim jacket. I squinted to get a better look, but couldn't see his face. I caught shadowy movement as a second person shifted just outside of my narrow field of vision.

Then the third person came into view — the pony-tailed man from the bank. Something glinted in his hand — a gun.

"Get down!" I whispered. I dragged Kitty with me and ducked behind the fridge.

The sounds of a scuffle came next, crashing, things falling, glass breaking, something big slamming into a wall.

The pony-tailed man barked, "This has gone too far. This —"

We scrambled back just as a shot rang out.

One of the doors splintered near its base. Fred's body heaved as a new bullet entered somewhere in his midsection. The refrigerator hissed out gasses.

"Jeeze," I whispered and hiccupped.

A siren wailed in the distance.

We heard footsteps running away, then the living room was quiet. A few seconds later came the throaty roar of a motorcycle.

FIVE

Kitty shoved her phone at me. "I told Ben we were pinned behind a dead person and that some fellows were shooting and whatnot." She wiggled the phone. "He wants to talk to you."

I took the phone. "Hello?"

"Kate," Ben's voice was level, "the state police are on the way right now. Are you both all right?"

I nodded and hiccupped into the phone. I peered through the doors. Papers littered the floor and furniture and lamps lay on their sides. Everything seemed still.

"We're okay. We're barricaded in, and whoever was here, they left."

"Stay in there," Ben said.

"They were looking for something." I tried to catch my breath.

"Okay. Just stay put. I'm twenty minutes away. The state police will get to you in half that."

We hunkered in to wait, and Ben kept me on the line. He had me describe the men in detail, prodding me with questions about height, weight, and what little of their features we saw.

The siren grew louder and wound down, then came footsteps across the porch.

I peeked out. An officer identified himself and asked if we were okay. He shoved at the doors, and Fred's nose flattened against the fridge.

"Hang on," I said.

I tugged the leaking refrigerator toward me and tipped Fred away from the door. I got the doors open about a foot and eased around the big appliance. Stepping over Fred, I sidled through the space with Kitty behind me. I grabbed her elbow and helped her through.

"Phew, that was something." Kitty straightened her fez and patted at her frizzled hair.

Another officer stuck his head into the kitchen. He stared down at Fred's body.

"Oh boy. It's all yours, Zowicki." He shook his head and, gun drawn, strode into the bedroom.

A pudgy man carrying a yellow tackle box crossed the living room. He wore street clothes but sported a state police seal over the breast pocket of his vinyl jacket. Booties covered his shoes, and he wore surgical gloves. A transparent paper shower cap covered his bald head.

The man lifted a laminated ID badge from a chain around his neck. Kitty read it.

"Elvis Zowicki?" she said.

"You skipped the Presley part. It's Elvis-Presley, the whole name — hyphenated. Most people just call me The King."

"I just bet Mercury is in retrograde," Kitty muttered.

The King produced a camera from his tackle box. He stuck his head through the doors.

"You've got to be kidding." He snapped a picture of Fred.

He bent over the body, lifted his camera, and clicked again, using his flash. "I was told this guy was shot. Looks like he had the bejeesus whacked out of him with a major kitchen appliance."

"That was us," Kitty said.

The King let the camera drop around his neck and glared at us. "*You* two did this?" His eyes narrowed and seemed to sink into his doughy face. "You here for the Sausage Festival?"

"Good Godfreys! You think we did this on

purpose?" Kitty took a few steps toward him.

Elvis-Presley put his hand up. "Stay back. You've ruined a perfectly good crime scene. Ruined it! And abusing a corpse is a criminal offense."

I patted the air between us. "Elvis, you see there were these guys here. One of them had a gun —"

"I told you." Elvis lifted a camera and flashed another picture with the strobe aimed in our direction. "It's the whole name or The King."

Kitty threw her hands up. "Oh, for pity's sake!"

Elvis-Presley worked the fridge back from where it was blocking the kitchen door and stepped over Fred. He pulled a giant canister off his tool belt and slapped it on the floor between us.

"Do not cross this threshold, or I'll use my riot unit." He prodded the body. "Sickos . . ."

Kitty started toward him. "I'll give you sicko —"

I grabbed her arm and pulled her deeper into the living room. "He's forensics, like *CSI* on TV."

"That's a *CSI* person?" Kitty said. "I don't believe it. A bald Elvis wannabe in a shower cap? They're always so sexy on the shows, and they have such nice equipment and whatnot."

As if on cue, our very own cop with the nice equipment strode through the door and pulled off his sunglasses. His eyes met mine, and my engine gave a little involuntary rumble. Even though we'd known each other since we were five, even though I'd married Andy by mistake and divorced him on purpose, Ben Williamson's arresting blue-gray eyes were still hotwired directly to my starter.

Ben's eyes, more gray than blue today, swept past us to Fred's body, then back to me. "Whoa. That's ugly."

The crime tech stood up. "This body's a mess, Ben." He jabbed an accusing finger in our direction. "Apparently, these women get off on abusing corpses. I'll have to bag this guy and take him back to the morgue to sort things out."

Elvis-Presley gave us a filthy look, adjusted his shower cap over the tips of his ears, and headed out of the apartment door.

"Ben," I grabbed his arm and pulled him away from the body. "We didn't —"

"Wait." Ben stepped close, to me. He rested his hands on my shoulders and looked me in the eyes. "Are you all right?"

I felt a tingle run through me. I nodded.

He looked at Kitty. "Are you okay?"

"Fine. It's been quite a day." Kitty trembled a bit and clutched my Stuart Weitzmans with bone-white knuckles.

Ben led Kitty to the couch, got her some water, and motioned me to follow him out to the porch.

"What are you two doing here, anyway? Aren't you supposed to be at the bank?" Ben jerked a thumb in Fred's direction. "With him?"

I took a deep breath. "Ben, we were at the bank when —"

A voice came from the bedroom. "Sheriff, you might want to see this."

Kitty and I gave Elvis-Presley our prints while Ben talked to the investigators in the other room. We watched Elvis load Fred's body onto a cart and wheel it across the porch on its way to that big Graceland in the sky.

"It seems Walter was a war hero," Ben called from the bedroom. "And whatever those guys wanted — they wanted it pretty bad. This place is a mess."

I wiped my inky fingers on a tissue, then picked my way around old-man socks and underpants, overturned drawers, and a pile of loafers and wingtips. Kitty followed.

Ben pointed to matching shadow boxes above the headboard. They held several medals. The rest of the room looked like the aftermath of a tornado — even the mattress had been dragged to the floor.

"Medals for marksmanship," Ben said. "World War Two and Korea, both. He could've shot his nephew, no question." Ben turned to me. "What were you doing here again?"

"We were at the bank —" I said

"You think my current Salsa partner could be a killer?" Kitty fanned herself. "First the bank robbery, now this! I feel just like Faye Dunaway in *Bonnie and Clyde*."

Ben looked at Kitty, then at me. His dark brows knitted together. "What's she talking about?"

She ignored him and said to me, "I guess we're lucky he used that banana at the bank."

Ben's deep voice rose up in pitch. "What bank? What banana? Kate, what's she talking about?"

"The bank got robbed this morning, and Walter did it, and Walter had my Stuart Weitzman boots. So that's how we ended up here and found Fred."

Ben stared at me from under furrowed brows.

Sheesh. I tried to tell the guy for the last hour, and it had to come out like that.

Ben swiveled his head back and forth between us. "No one reported a robbery."

"Trust me," I said. "Walter robbed Mudd Lake Savings at nine-thirty this morning."

"Kate and I almost got the money back. We were this close." Kitty squeezed her fingers together. "Our bank deposits, too. But there was this horrid trooper. His manners were absolutely abysmal."

"Wait! The bank deposits? He stole the deposits? Before you made them?" He took a step backward and stared at me again. "Argh!"

Ben bent his head and banged it against the doorjamb. "The county commissioner's going to toss me off the freaking lighthouse."

"The whole thing was very weird." I waved my hands in the air. "Surreal. Like the teller didn't take Walter seriously — until he used his gun."

"Actually, he used a banana," Kitty said.

"And why didn't they report it?" I looked at Kitty. "And that man from the bank came here, and poor dead Fred, and Walter was wearing his pajamas . . ."

"Stop!" Ben thudded his head into the wood again. "Criminy, this had to happen in an election year."

47

"The election's months away," I said.

The top of his head still pressed against the door frame, Ben turned his face sideways and looked at me. "Albert Schwenck's going to have a field day with this."

"Ben, darling, no worries." Kitty flapped her hand. "Nobody will vote for Albert in the primary. He's a buffoon, besides he has visible nose hairs."

Ben straightened and shook his head sadly. "Mudd Lake was due to get a commendation from the governor for fifteen years with no murders. Kate, I'm glad you moved back here. *Really* glad." Ben's gray eyes pinned mine and my engine gave a purr. "But you're like a crime . . . *magnet* or something. You attract it. You come back from Chicago, and poof! We've got bad guys up the ying-yang."

He made an upward poking motion to show how the ying-yang felt.

"That's a coincidence," I said.

"I blame Mercury," Kitty said.

Ben turned to the door frame and resumed his thudding.

"Anyway, the governor still likes us." I turned my palms toward Walter's brass ceiling fixture. "She came to the Fur Ball and squeezed the mustard on the World's Largest Sausage and everything."

I cleared my throat. It had come out more lame than I expected.

Ben sighed and straightened again. He ran a hand through his wavy black hair. "I was dreaming to think I could do this job part time. I'm going to drop out of dental school."

I caught my breath. "No! You need to follow your dream, be a dentist. A sheriff and a dentist. You can do both, just like your father did."

Ben shook his head. "Before the drill accident, my dad used to say what a weight Mudd Lake's teeth became when combined with all the responsibility of keeping the peace."

I stroked Ben's arm. "Your father left some mighty big shoes to fill."

"And teeth," Kitty said.

I shot her a warning look. Kitty's production choice of *Little Shop of Horrors* with its sadistic dentist had made Ben a little touchy of late.

Ben glanced out the window at a passing trooper. "Schwenck's got a slogan — *Williamsons fill molars not jails.*"

"Albert runs a septic tank company — I'm sure you could come up with an appropriate retort," Kitty said.

"The festival money. And a murder." Ben

rubbed his forehead. "I don't even know where to start."

I peeked under the bed. Nothing but dust bunnies. I straightened and made my voice sound confident. "We'll turn this around. We have to. We'll find Walter and those other guys. Recover the money."

Ben rolled his eyes. "I'm dead meat."

After the kitchen, I felt a bond with poor Fred. "I can help with the murder investigation —"

Ben snorted.

I gasped, stared at him, then shot off a snort myself. "That's it! I took your stupid auxiliary deputy job — I wanted to be helpful — even though the uniform sucked, and the shoes were all wrong for me." My voice climbed in pitch. "I did crowd control at the Festival. I gave stupid pooper-scoop warnings for the stupid Bow-wow Waddle! Things go sideways and first thing, you want to give up school. I offer to help and you — you *snort* at me?"

Ben took a step toward me. "Kate —"

"Don't think I don't know what that snort meant." I stuck my chin in the air. I sounded petulant, but I didn't give a rat's patootie. "I am a very competent person, and I have an affinity for law enforcement, and you know it."

50

So what if that affinity consisted of arresting Ben with toy handcuffs and a Deputy Dawg badge when we were six?

Ben pressed his lips together in a straight line. It curled around the edges.

In keeping with my petulant theme, I jutted my jaw out and swiveled my head away.

Ben touched my shoulder. "Wait, I know you're competent. I —"

We heard a toilet flush, and the bathroom door opened. Kitty crossed between us, a feather-trimmed negligee draped over one arm.

My jaw dropped.

Feathers molted as Kitty hoisted the flamingo-pink chiffon toward Ben. "Mind if I take this and Kate's boots? It's my costume for the finale. I watch *CSI,* so I know it's a crime scene and all, but those guys said they were done."

I yanked my eyes away from the transparent fabric. "I didn't know you were sleeping with him."

Kitty blew a feather away from her chin. "Oh, I slept with him a few times. It's the staying awake part that gave us the fits."

Ben's face turned the same pink as Kitty's negligee. After squirming a few seconds, he flipped his notepad to a fresh page, cleared his throat, and asked about the bank.

I gave him a terse statement.

I could only do petulant for so long. It made my head hurt. "Can I come with you? I have some questions for —"

"Uh-oh." Kitty looked at her watch. "We're going to be late for rehearsal."

Just when I thought it couldn't get any worse.

Six

Ben headed to Mudd Lake Savings, and we drove the mile or so across town to the Egyptian Theatre. I parked the Land Yacht in front of our decaying, somewhat embarrassing family business, and Kitty draped her negligee over her arm and hopped out. She slipped between the painted plaster statues of Isis and Osiris and disappeared into the lobby.

Above me, the pyramid-shaped marquee's big black letters shouted, "THANK YOU MUDD LAKE FOR A GREAT BENEFIT." I winced. I stood outside the car and debated going up the wooden exterior steps to my apartment above the theatre, maybe hiding under my bed — but I'd only delay the inevitable.

I walked under the marquee and stepped into the lobby. I inhaled the faint, nutty smell of years of popcorn overlaid with the musty odor of old building — the smell of home.

I adjusted a carpet runner over the missing floor tiles on the way past the concession stand and pulled open the first set of doors to the auditorium. I stopped halfway down the main aisle.

On stage, the Audrey Two, the massive man-eating plant puppet, skulked and swaggered to the strains of *Little Shop*'s big number, "Suppertime."

The puppet's gargantuan foam rubber jaws opened and closed to mouth words. She moved across the stage, roots trailing from her flowerpot. Her big alien head bent, and she showed sharp-looking rubber teeth.

I heaved in a breath and gazed up at the inverted stained-glass pyramid sparkling over the seating area. As a kid, I'd thought this Viennese chandelier, bought by my grandfather in 1927, had magical powers. But then, I'd thought this whole theatre had such powers, and Kitty had, too.

A flicker of memory ran like an old celluloid in my mind — I was five years old, watching my parents wave goodbye. Three hours later their plane and another had collided over the Grand Canyon, and they vaporized.

Poof — a giant cosmic vanishing act.

And I came to the Egyptian, to Kitty. She'd woven her spell, and the magic had worked. Thanks to my own personal Auntie Mame, I'd survived. I'd even thrived. I scanned the ornate ceiling plaster for new cracks and came back to earth in time to see the Audrey Two's jaws snap shut mid-sentence.

"Hey!" Kitty hollered from center stage.

Scotty Forsythe's rich baritone trailed off in the middle of a verse. The Audrey Two's head drooped to the boards. Her felt cerebellum split open and a wiry guy dressed in more black than a Ninja movie extra emerged.

"It's about time you got here." Leo, our lead puppeteer, pulled off his black knit hat and stuffed it in the rear pocket of his black jeans.

I passed some cast members seated in the first few rows and felt their gazes on me as I climbed the steps.

"You've got our money, right?" Leo came around the front of the big puppet and stood hands on hips.

I stepped back. "I need a few more days. We ran into a snag and —"

"I knew it!" A second puppeteer, Ross, wriggled out of Audrey's green foam-stuffed root. He turned to Leo. "She's a deadbeat."

I straightened. "I am not!"

"Are too!" Ross shook his finger at me.

"Our first installment's due today. No pay, no work!" Leo hollered.

"You boys need to understand." Kitty stepped over the Audrey Two's dead root. "We were robbed while at the bank."

The cast members gave off audible gasps. A murmur rose up from the seats and spread to the knot of Players clustered on the stage.

"Not the benefit money!"

"It wasn't deposited?"

"We worked so hard!"

"CracklePops will never give us the grant, now." The man who played Mushnik, the florist, stuffed his hands in his pockets and hung his head.

Kitty's best friend, the show's director, Verna Wilson, stepped out from the wings. Verna smoothed her polka-dot housedress and patted her tight bluish curls. She blinked behind shiny bifocals and looked from Kitty to me.

"Oh, my stars! Are you two all right?" Verna's brow wrinkled with concern.

Kitty leaned close to her friend and provided her with whispered details. She patted Verna's dotted sleeve. "It was quite a day."

"Oh, my stars," Verna said again.

Kitty smiled at the assembled group. "No worries. The CracklePops Foundation will love our show."

I said, "And we'll get the money back. I'm working with the sheriff —"

Someone groaned.

"Who said that?" I narrowed my eyes and squinted at the first few rows of seats.

Verna moved to the footlights. "Don't you folks worry."

"I'm worried." Milton Huff, our insurance agent, stepped forward. He ran the sound equipment. "Too bad you went so cheap," he said. "No insurance coverage for things like this."

More murmurs and a few swear words.

"I just knew it!" Leo stepped forward and poked a finger at my chest. "You can't afford professionals like us. Crappy insurance and no money. Deadbeat!" He looked at the other puppeteer. "We're outta here, right, Ross?"

"Wait." I patted the air between us. "I'll pay you!"

"Now?" Ross wanted to know.

I smoothed imaginary ruffled feathers in the tense atmosphere. "A day or two —"

"No way." Leo shook his head and pointed at the boards in front of his feet. "Now."

Ross sneered. "She can't manage a theatre. This place is a dump. The whole thing's gonna go belly-up."

Leo and Ross looked at each other, then squawked in unison, "We quit."

Leo tossed me his knit hat and started down the steps.

The murmurs from the crowd started again.

Kitty beamed her best thousand-watt smile at the Players. "You folks are actors. Volunteers. *True* theatre lovers. You needn't worry about trivia like this."

She brushed a dismissive hand at Ross and Leo, then at the empty green root costume.

"*Anyone* can wear that thing."

I poked myself in the chest. "And I've operated theatre puppets before. I have experience . . . um . . . from Chicago!"

Was that me? What the hell was I thinking?

Kitty stopped breathing. She stared at me, wide-eyed, then sucked in a gust of air and fired up her smile. "She will be smashing in the big Audrey Two. Simply smashing." She swept her hand again at the puppeteers. "Go on boys, you're fired. Tah-tah."

Leo started down the aisle then turned. He made his thumb and finger into an "L" shape and plastered it to his forehead.

"Loser!"

"You're the loser." I banged an imaginary "L" against my own forehead.

God, he was right. I was pathetic. I looked at the dozing Audrey Two. I'd just found my own personal hell.

In a voice that always reminded me of crinkly cellophane, Verna said, "Rehearsal tomorrow, same as always."

I sighed.

One by one, the Players gathered scripts and duffle bags before trooping toward the lobby doors.

"No worries, my talented darlings," Kitty called after them, "the Egyptian is as stable as ever."

Someone wailed, and there was talk of heading to the bar for tequila shots.

Once the three of us were alone Kitty said, "My Godfreys! What were you thinking?"

What the hell *was* I thinking?

I sucked in a deep breath and tilted my face toward the light bars shining above us. I felt lightheaded and saw spots when I looked back at Kitty and Verna.

I blew out air and shook my head. "I honestly don't know. Maybe I had some sort of seizure or something."

Verna turned to me. "Can you manage it, dear? Can you operate the Audrey Two?"

"Uh . . . well." I eyed the droopy alien plant.

"Kate played a shepherd in the Christmas nativity play once," Kitty said. "She did use a puppet. That part is true — her Lamb Chop puppet. She was nine." Kitty shook her head and patted my shoulder. "I need a martini." She tossed her negligee over one shoulder and headed for the greenroom.

Verna's twinkly blue eyes drilled into me.

Beads of cold sweat bloomed on my forehead and upper lip. My stomach felt like I'd swallowed a clenched fist. I remembered that long-ago Christmas play. Paralyzed by stage fright, I'd begun to hiccup as soon as I'd walked on stage. People had giggled, and that made me hiccup more. This giggling and hiccupping built back and forth to a momentous crescendo, and I upchucked all over the baby Jesus.

"Puppets. How hard can that be?" I said and hiccupped.

Kitty reappeared with an imitation silver tray from the prop shelf. It held two iced teas and a stemmed martini glass. She set the tray on the plywood florist's counter center stage.

Verna plopped down on the stool next to her and fanned herself with the flyer from Splotski's Theatre Supplies.

We owed them three grand for the puppet rental.

Kitty rummaged around beneath the counter and produced a box of Godiva chocolates.

"Poor Fred," Verna said. "And Walter! Do you think Walter killed Fred? His own nephew? And he's robbing the bank again?" Verna shook her head. "Did they change his medication or something?"

Kitty caught Verna's free hand. She squeezed. "Now, darling, let's not burden Kate with old news. I don't think Walter's a killer, but I'm still breaking up with him." Kitty took a sip of her martini and swirled the tiny silver dagger that impaled two olives, another prop, this one from Kitty's fourth movie, *Dastardly Dames,* circa 1961.

"Robbing the bank *again?*" I lifted an eyebrow and skirted around the Audrey Two. "Back up a sec, ladies."

"It was nothing, really." Kitty picked up a chocolate and stuffed it in her mouth.

Of course. Chiffon's blasé attitude that morning suddenly made sense. "Walter's robbed the bank before, right?"

"Oh, yes, dear, several times." Verna put the Splotski's brochure on the counter.

"Kitty, you knew this guy robbed banks? And you dated him anyway?" She was on her second piece of chocolate, a caramel, but it couldn't last forever.

I waited.

"I've been trying to date in my age group." Kitty wiggled a crescent of goo-filled chocolate my way. "Any idea how hard it is to find fellows over seventy who can Salsa?"

I groaned.

Kitty cleared Godiva from her throat. "Walter had this little prescription snafu a while back. You know how the wrong medication can affect the elderly."

"That's right," Verna said. "A couple of years ago, Walter took to robbing Mudd Lake Savings. It was the oddest thing."

"I think it had to do with his bad plumbing and whatnot." Kitty took another bite of chocolate and chased it with a sip of martini. "Some kind of prostate pill that disagreed."

Verna nodded. "First thing in the morning, every day for a week. Folks were all a-twitter about drug interactions over at the Senior Center."

Both women lived in the Center's apartments. With the exception of the annual Sausage Festival, it was Mudd Lake's social hub, a depressing factoid for those of us under sixty-five.

"Maybe it's those piddle drugs again." Kitty held the Godiva box out for Verna.

"Does Ben know about this?" I took a sip of my tea and held the cool glass to my forehead.

"No, I don't believe so." Verna lifted a dark chocolate. She spotted Kitty's nail mark on the bottom and replaced it. "Only some of us at the Senior Center knew, and, of course, the folks at the bank."

"Fred wouldn't let them report it," Kitty said.

"Fred picked the money up on his lunch hour." Verna shook her head. "And the bank was always empty when he robbed it."

I made a face. "Not reporting your own bank robbery — I'm not sure what law it breaks, but it's got to be out there."

"Nancy wanted it kept quiet," Kitty said. She leaned forward. "I heard Nancy and Fred were getting a divorce."

"Nancy who?" I looked from Verna to Kitty and felt my neck muscles tense up.

"Fred's wife," Kitty said. "She's the money behind the bank. It's her family business."

Dots connected in my head. "Nancy von Dickel is Fred's wife?"

"Nancy von Dickel-Schnebbly. Walter is her blood uncle," Kitty said. "You and Nancy used to be inseparable. Whatever happened?"

"Can't recall." I stared at the pillaged Godiva box.

"Nancy von Dickel, huh? Great." I kept my voice flat, then reached for Kitty's martini and sucked down a big slug.

Twenty minutes later, I walked Kitty and Verna to the Land Yacht and retrieved my Stuart Weitzman boots. I headed to the side of the Egyptian and climbed the stairs to my apartment. Around ankle height, a damp black nose smudged the sidelight window by my front door. A flash of stringy brown fur streaked low across the glass and disappeared. I stepped inside and heard tags clinking toward the kitchen.

"Most dogs run to greet a person," I called.

Silence. Then crunching.

"Had my Purina already, thanks!" I said.

More crunching.

I followed the sound to the kitchen. Ernie, my shaggy, scruffy, dachshund-poodle mix, regarded me from under bushy eyebrows. He buried his nose in his food dish. His wispy tail swished back and forth, but he emitted a garbled growl. He glared, then snarfed up more kibbles.

I pictured the index card clipped to his cage a year ago: "Special Needs," and under that a typed list that included food neurosis, separation anxiety, mood swings, paranoia, and rampant disobedience. Across it, someone had scrawled in angry red letters, *"biter!"*

But then those liquid brown eyes had locked on mine, and that stringy tail had thumped out a drumbeat of hope. And none of that other stuff mattered. I took him home.

I squatted on my heels and waited while Ernie gulped down the last of that morning's leftover breakfast. He finished, then barreled toward me on stubby legs, his pennant of a tail waving wildly. He leapt into my arms, slurped at my chin, and let out an exuberant, yodel-like bark. He ran his nose across my Stuart Weitzmans.

"Hey, don't slime the merchandise," I said holding them out of reach.

In the bedroom I slipped into fresh jeans and a sweater and parked my Stuart Weitzmans in the oversized wardrobe, along with my freshly wiped Jimmy Choos. I eyed my collection and chose a black suede Etienne Aigner ankle boot with a decorative gold loop on the side.

I wouldn't call myself a shoe-freak or anything, and I only buy on sale. Okay, so I buy dirt-cheap, but there's something about a well-dressed foot. It's one of the joys of being female, right up there with good hair days, black mascara, and cherry-flavored lip gloss.

Across the room on the nightstand, my answering machine blinked. I pressed the button.

"Kate, Joe Splotski here. I'm gonna need my puppet money up front after all. Leo, the puppet guy, tells me you're a deadbeat, and your show's gonna flop." There was a pause. "No offense or anything. Cough up the money or the puppets. You've got forty-eight hours."

I frowned at the machine and punched erase.

Great. Just great.

I clipped Ernie's leash to his harness. I avoided the inside stairs that led past the stage and the Audrey Two and headed outside to my landing. I followed Ernie's long shaggy body down the stairs.

Seven

Three blocks away, the Sausage Festival was in full swing, and Lighthouse Park teemed with people.

"Maybe you could do it?" I said over the din of the Oom-Pah-Pah tent. "Run the Audrey Two? Performing doesn't make *you* barf on any religious icons or anything."

My best friend Charlene plunked a heavily laden tray between us on the picnic table. "I can't do it. I've got a big trial the end of the month — more public defender work. You're welcome to come by and barf on the prosecutor, though."

Charlene tucked a wisp of dark hair back into her ponytail and worked her way onto the bench across from me. We sat surrounded by about two hundred other sausage revelers. The spicy, redolent smell of the grilling meats hung in the air and permeated everything throughout the massive yellow-and-white striped tent.

I reached for my Italian Torpedo Pepper and Onion Sausage Surprise. "I said I was buying, but bless you."

Under our feet, Ernie settled in with his bowl of sausage crumbles. Charlene poured beer from a plastic pitcher into our cups.

I smiled at her as she handed me my beer. A good friend knows when you need someone to listen to your troubles. A best friend knows when to shove you a pile of greasy food with an alcohol chaser.

"I don't know why I'm worried about running the puppets anyway," I said. "Without the loan we're sunk. We need three grand just to pay Splotski's, and I have no idea where to even get that." I put my beer down and hung my head between my hands. "I can't believe this happened."

"Fred liked the Egyptian. The bank will replace him," Charlene said, "but who knows when, or even if, his replacement will approve the loan."

I thought of Fred, dead on that tiny kitchen floor, and gazed at my sausage.

"Maybe you should cancel the Crackle-Pops Foundation." Charlene took a sip of beer.

I rubbed my temples and willed away the headache that threatened to set up shop. "We cancel, we'll never get them again."

"We finally get the Foundation interested, get a chance at real money, and this has to happen." Charlene shook her head. "This is looking like a typical Mudd Lake Players disaster."

"Walter von Dickel isn't working alone, that much is clear," I said. "If I can find him, maybe I can somehow get our money back."

"Oh boy," Charlene rolled her eyes to the bare light bulbs strung overhead. "I can see where this is going."

"You know everything about this town," I said. "Spill the beans on Walter and the Schnebblys." I bit into my greasy, spicy sandwich and waited.

"Let's see . . . ," Charlene brushed a breadcrumb off her I "heart" the Constitution sweatshirt and started talking.

By the time we finished our sausages and beer, I knew that Nancy had in fact filed for divorce a week ago.

"Fred was staying at Walter's," Charlene said. "Sleeping on the couch. Even though they were only related by marriage, Walter and Fred seemed really close." Charlene waved to a couple headed for the grassy area in front of the band, then looked back at me. "Rumor has it, Fred had a girlfriend."

The polka band started up with a wheezy

staccato melody. People from eight to eighty formed a circle in front of the stage. They flapped elbows, waddled, and squatted to the music.

I yelled over the blatting of the tuba. "Fifteen years I lived in Chicago, I never once saw the Chicken Dance. I'm not sure I missed it."

Charlene grinned and slid the remains of our beer pitcher to four grateful men sitting at the next table.

"My mom has double-chunk chocolate chip cookies at her booth." Charlene stood up. "Come on."

"Sausage, beer and cookies, maybe I'll get through this day after all," I said.

We passed concessions that ranged from the exotic ouzo-soaked Greek loukanika at the Flaming Sausage to the lowly hotdog from Dave's Dogs'n Suds. From his spot tucked under my arm, Ernie's long nose twitched with aroma-induced bliss.

We followed Charlene through the crowd. A pudgy, bald man wearing lederhosen and a tall, floppy, Dr. Seuss top-hat dragged Charlene's mom, Edna, past us toward the dance floor.

"Can't miss the Chicken Dance," Edna Lebonowitz squawked over the noise. She slapped her elbows against her plump body.

"Cover for me!"

Behind the counter at the Mama's Deli concession, Juan, Mama's cook, ladled home-made sauerkraut over a grilled kielbasa while people jammed around him waving food tickets.

"These poker people. They're nuts," he called to us over the cacophony of tuba, sizzling meat, and sausage revelers sucking down their third or fourth beers.

I tied Ernie's leash to the heavy tent pole behind the booth, and he crawled to a protected spot under the table. Charlene took the ladle from Juan and loaded kraut while I collected food tickets and called out orders.

"Is so crazy that we have to come here all week." Juan flapped a delicate wrist toward the sea of Chicken Dancers. "I hate this stupid Chorizo Festival."

"Sausage Festival," Charlene said.

"Yeah. Yeah. Whatever. The ugly-man festival, that's what it is. And they all winners! I never see so many ugly men in one place."

"It's the lederhosen," I said. I dropped the tickets I'd taken into a large glass jar and collected two more. "Nobody looks good in lederhosen."

A waiter from the Flaming Sausage walked

past with a metal tray of loukanika. He flicked a lighter and flame rolled over the tray, causing everybody in the general vicinity to duck.

"Opa!" he hollered.

"Stupid Greek sausage. Stupid poker dancing. Stupid festival. Crazy people and drunks." Juan shook his head and half-heartedly spun a dozen or so kielbasa on the grill rods.

The speakers blared, and we heard the voice of the lead singer in the Polka band. "We'd like to dedicate the next song to Fred Schnebbly, one of Mudd Lake's own, felled today in a violent crime."

The band rolled into "In Heaven They Have No Beer." The pudgy man in the Dr. Seuss hat tugged Mrs. Lebonowitz deeper into the dancers. I glanced toward the entrance. I clutched a food ticket in mid-air and froze. The tent continued to explode with noisy polka music and chatter.

"No way," I whispered.

Walter von Dickel stood in the opening backlit by the strobe of the midway lights. He looked like Clint Eastwood in some old Spaghetti Western, except the saloon always got really quiet when Clint Eastwood came in, and no one noticed Walter but me.

Clint never wore what looked to be a

triple-XL tie-dyed Phish T-shirt, either. The T-shirt hung huge on Walter's bony frame and grazed his knees. Walter's jeans looked to be four sizes too big, and he still wore his floppy slippers. An outline of something gun-like poked through from his pocket.

The heat of adrenaline steamed away what little beer buzz I had like so much water off a hot griddle. A thousand thoughts shot through my mind at once.

"No way!" I yelled.

I jabbed Charlene with my elbow and pointed. "That's him! That's Walter von Dickel."

Charlene dropped her ladle and stared. "Oh my God."

Walter's glance darted from booth to booth. He spotted the cash table. He shoved his hand in his pocket and shuffled toward it. A woman tore tickets off a fat roll while another loaded cash into a metal box.

I jabbed my finger at Walter. "You hold it. You hold it right there!" I hollered.

I ran out from behind the counter and pushed my way through the milling crowd. Charlene followed me.

Juan wiped his hands on his apron. "Hey! You're not leaving me alone with these poker peoples. I come with you."

He followed us.

We were twenty feet away and swimming upstream against the crowd when Walter swooped in and grabbed the cashbox. He stuffed the metal container under one arm and headed straight for us.

"You crazy old fart!" I yelled. With Juan and Charlene flanking me, I blocked Walter's path

"Outta my way, you!" Walter shoved a hand into Juan's chest and latched onto the top of Juan's apron. He yanked Juan to him.

"Help!" Juan let out a squeal. He shoved at Walter. "Get away from me, ugly man!"

Walter swung Juan into my chest and let go. I rocked backward on my two-and-a-half-inch chunk heels.

"Oh, no you don't!" I dove for Walter and snatched at the bottom of his T-shirt. I missed.

Charlene swooped in behind him, but Walter skirted around a huge Greek waiter with a tray full of sausage. The waiter stepped forward and flicked his Bic. Heat and flame exploded in front of us with an eyebrow-singing whoosh.

"Opa!" the Greek guy bellowed.

"Opa!" the crowd hollered and cheered.

I scrambled around the fiery tray and lunged for Walter who grabbed a plastic beer pitcher off the table and whipped it behind him. Beer sloshed everywhere on the crowd but mostly on me, soaking through my sweater and onto my chest. The pitcher tumbled to the ground beside us, and Charlene stumbled over it.

"Arrgh!" she croaked.

"Right back atcha over there, eh!" a guy behind me yelled. A pitcher flew above my head, and more beer sloshed over my shoulder and soaked my hair. A bratwurst sailed past my right ear.

A gangly teenager climbed on a picnic table and winged a paper plate Frisbee-like, sending French fries everywhere. "All right!" he yelled. "Cool! Food fi-ight!"

The band redoubled their effort on "In Heaven They Have No Beer." Sausage and beer flew everywhere around us.

Walter cut into the line of dancers. He pushed between the Cat-in-the-Hat man and Edna Lebonowitz and shoved his way through the center of the six-piece Bavarian band. Instruments and musicians clattered and tumbled into a heap. Charlene's mom staggered, and her plump body rocked. She tilted backward into the stage area.

"Cheese-n-rice all Friday!" Mrs. Lebonowitz hollered. Her feet flew out from under her, and she went down.

"Whoa, Mom!"

Charlene jumped into the chaos and grabbed one of her mother's arms. Juan grabbed the other, and together they pulled Mrs. Lebonowitz off the flailing tuba player.

"Jesus, Mary, Jehosaphat!" Edna Lebonowitz crossed herself. She watched Walter cut through the pandemonium to the exit. "What the hell was that?"

"Go! Go get him!" Charlene yelled. She tightened her grip on her mom's pudgy arm. "That man's a fruitcake!" Charlene raised her head and hollered, "Walter von Dickel, don't expect me to defend your gnarly ass when Kate catches you either!"

Walter shot out the exit and onto the midway. Slippers flapping, he made tracks through the crowd. Drenched in beer, my heart pounding, I ran behind him. We circled St. Agatha's casino tent and headed toward the midway. I swiped for the flapping Phish shirt and missed. I pushed through the startled onlookers, but Walter wove around a knot of young teens and broke out in front. I spotted him ten yards ahead, weaving through the line for the Ferris wheel. He glanced back, then cut sideways behind the Zipper ride.

"Hold it!" I gasped for breath. I pushed my hand against my aching side and wheezed, "Stop . . . right there!"

Walter hesitated, trotted a few feet, then bolted around the corner behind the food trailers.

"Wait!" I rounded the corn-dog stand. "Halt!" I leaned against the trailer and panted. "How the hell old are you anyway?"

Walter slowed. I huffed up a breath and staggered after him wobbling on my too-tall heels.

I dodged a strolling couple holding hands and came face to face with Walter. He stood dead-center between the funnel cakes and elephant ears. He wasn't even breathing very hard.

"You!" he said in a hoarse whisper. He grabbed my wrist and shoved a twenty dollar bill into my hand. "Take this!"

He pushed my fingers into a tight fist and patted it.

I lunged for his shoulder. "Only about five hundred to go —"

"No! Get away!"

He slammed the heel of his hand under my chin in a sharp uppercut. My neck snapped back, and I lost my balance. I stumbled backward into the sawdust and collapsed.

A few seconds later, I scrambled to my feet and scooted behind Flossie's Funnel Cakes. I rolled my neck around. It snapped and cracked like CracklePops cereal in cold milk.

I swore like an extremely ticked-off sailor with a potentially damaged high-heel and shoved the twenty into my pocket. I rubbed my aching jaw.

Beer and sauerkraut clung in clumps to my sweater and backside, and I smelled like a German restaurant's garbage can.

I wiggled my foot, the heel seemed fine. I tested it again. It held.

A man had been murdered, I'd been manhandled by an indefatigable grandpa with a bad prostate, and I might have ruined a pair of deeply discounted high-end boots. The lights flickered on the Egyptian's future, and the future of Mudd Lake's teeth hung in the balance. One thought, one goal, filled my mind and eclipsed all others. I wanted to find Walter von Dickel and choke him with his bathrobe sash until he coughed up our money.

Working my jaw back and forth, I limped back to the Oom-Pah-Pah tent.

EIGHT

Ben took crime reports and closed the festival half an hour early so the volunteer fire department could hose down the tent. On the way home he walked beside me, while Ernie snuffled from shrub to shrub out in front of us.

I looked out at the lighthouse silhouetted against the moonlight on the Lake Michigan shoreline, then we passed an Albert Schwenck campaign poster tacked to a phone pole. I winced. Albert sneered at us from the poster. The real-live Albert had to be loving this.

"I almost had him," I muttered. "Stupid flaming sausage guys. Stupid Walter."

"I'm surprised he got away from you on the midway," Ben said. "You know he's eighty-two."

I narrowed my eyes and cut them at Ben.

Ben held his fingers up. "Hey! He probably works out or something."

We passed another Schwenck poster. They were plastered to every pole.

Ben took my elbow, and turned me to face him. "You're not still mad are you? About the snort thing?"

I read the concern in his gorgeous eyes.

I sighed and rolled my neck back and forth. "I guess not," I said. "You knew Walter robbed Mudd Lake Savings before, right?"

Ben nodded and shoved his hands in his pockets. He hunched his broad shoulders. "I found out when I took the report at the bank. Chiffon didn't want to admit it at first. I guess Nancy Schnebbly hushed it up the other times."

"Nancy *von Dickel*-Schnebbly," I said

We were walking again. I reeled Ernie's extend-o-leash toward me, putting him out of range of a teasing tabby cat walking figure-eights ahead of us.

"Nancy von Dickel, yep, I know." Ben glanced over at me. "Kate, I've been thinking, I really could use your help on this."

I perked up. He was going to get my help whether he wanted it or not, but it was nice to be asked. "Sure. What do you need?"

"Visit Nancy von Dickel-Schnebbly tomorrow. She has a big financial motive to want Fred dead. See what you think of her as a suspect."

"I said I wanted to help, but *her?*" I wrinkled my nose. "One of those men at Walter's today, or maybe Walter himself, killed Fred. That's my theory." I swerved around a cherry branch hung low with blossoms.

Ben lifted a sweet-smelling limb out of our way. "Nancy could have hired those guys. She and her uncle might somehow be in cahoots on the robbery."

"Well, she is a thief . . ." I said.

Ben rolled his eyes. "Right," he said. "Go pay her an unofficial condolence call. You and Nancy were friends once."

"That was a long time ago." I made another face. "Want to practice your root canals on me first? Get me warmed up for my visit?"

"You're not still mad about the underpants, are you?" A hint of Ben's lopsided smile appeared, and mischief sparkled in his blue eyes. "That was twenty years ago. We were all fourteen."

I sighed. If I wanted to prove my mettle, here was my chance. "Okay, Nancy just traded divorce papers for a death certificate." We turned onto Main. "Good point."

"She's in the suspect line right behind Walter and the men at the apartment.

81

Maybe those goons took care of a problem divorce for Nancy, and Walter pulled a robbery to pay off the killers for her."

"Two robberies," I reminded him. "And why? Nancy could pay."

"Maybe Walter's crazy." Ben shrugged. "Or not . . . With Walter's history and his oddball behavior, they could mount a pretty strong insanity defense for the robberies. A short vacation at the bubble factory, and he'd be back on the streets."

Ben's radio crackled at his shoulder. The electronic sound of Eunice, Ben's under-sheriff, came through the speaker.

"All heck's breaking loose, boss. Some-body broke into Walter's apartment," she said. "Ransacked the place. They turned it upside down. I mean, what wasn't upside-down already."

I turned on my abused, but still sexy, high heel and headed in the direction of Ben's Tahoe. "Let's go."

"Whoa, there, Kojak. Remember that word, unofficial? Ice up your neck and jaw. Get some rest." Ben peeled a shred of kraut off my forehead.

"Can sauerkraut go bad? Is it even pos-sible?" I wrinkled my nose again. "I smell like the Oom-Pah-Pah tent."

"I like the Oom-Pah-Pah tent." Ben

moved closer. "I grew up with it."

We'd dated through most of high school and college. "I know exactly what you grew up with, and it had nothing to do with Oom-Pah-Pah."

He grinned, and those eyes glittered in the glow from the streetlight. He lifted another thread of sauerkraut off my sweater. "I'd better go deal with my newest disaster. Get back to me after you're done with Nancy."

Ben glanced around, then kissed me quickly but softly on the lips. A tingle ran through me, but I moved downwind and fanned the air between us.

Ben lifted an eyebrow. "I really love that tent."

He winked at me, and my heart did a little skip. I watched Ben's hips as he disappeared around the corner.

Tomorrow I'd find out everything Nancy von Dickel-Schnebbly knew. I'd show Ben some good detective work. I'd pump that woman like a sump in a flooded basement.

NINE

Ernie and I walked the remaining half-block home.

Next door to the Egyptian, we passed the Acadia Building's majestic granite Indians, and neon from Benny's Bail Bonds lent a rosy cast to the sidewalk. Bits of mica sparkled like tiny pink galaxies beneath my feet. To the west, moonlight skipped over Lake Michigan's choppy waters.

I looked up at the dark sign for Mama's Deli, Charlene's mother's place. She'd bounced back after her run-in with the tuba player, but Charlene and Juan had wanted to hover anyway. Above the Mama's sign loomed a black rectangle, the window to Charlene's law offices.

In front of the Egyptian, I kept watch while Ernie squatted. We understood each other. Part of my job occurred whenever he peed like a girl dog — I had his back.

Movement in the alley caught my eye.

Ernie straightened and stuck his wispy tail straight in the air. His long ears stiffened, and he rolled out a low growl. The events of the day skittered through my brain, and my heart stepped up its pace.

A garbage can clattered to its side, and the clanging echoed through the empty streets. Raccoon eyes glowed yellow in the dim aura from my porch light. The big animal tugged a chicken carcass from a ripped plastic garbage bag and sunk needle teeth into its fleshy thigh. He snapped the drumstick free and dragged it deeper into the shadows.

I blew out a breath.

Another shadow moved, and a big man in a Bill Clinton mask stepped out from under my stairs: the getaway car driver. I froze in my tracks and gulped.

Ernie growled so hard his ears wobbled. The hulking man took a step toward us. Ernie yapped, and his front feet flew off the ground. He looked like a fragile, over-protective wind-up toy.

I yanked the leash, scooped my little dog into my arms, and hugged him. I raised my voice over the frenzied barking. "Wh-wh-what are you doing here?"

The man said nothing. A paper blew across the empty alley. The place felt as desolate as something out of Kitty's old horror movies.

Finally Bill Clinton wiggled the rubbery mask and tilted his head back. He peered through the eye slits at me. His gruff voice came out muffled. "You cook and sing at popcorn, and iguana, bitch!"

I screwed my face up and looked at him. "Huh?"

He pulled the rubber mouth down and slid his head back in a further attempt to see.

"Damned thing," he muttered, "can't see for crap."

I squeezed Ernie and eased back around the capsized garbage can.

"Oh, no you don't!"

The big man let the mask snap back in place and lunged toward me. His arm shot out, and he clamped giant fingers tight around my wrist.

"Let go!" I tried to sound tough and unafraid, but my voice squeaked.

Ernie growled and snapped at the sleeve of Bill's denim jacket.

"You cook some sing, iguana!"

"I don't know what you're talking about! Hold the mask away from your mouth." I twisted my torso and wrenched my arm free. I shoved my chunky stacked heel into the big man's booted shin and squirmed away.

He stared at my heel, then spewed garbled profanities.

Tugging the mask down with one big hand, he lurched for me. "You took something, I want it!" He stumbled into the torn trash bag, and his boot slid over the greasy remains of the chicken carcass. The mask snapped against his chin. "Ship!" he yelled.

I backed up some more.

A loud chattering and hissing came from the alley behind the ersatz Bill Clinton. Headlight beams illuminated the raccoon's eyes as he glared at the squashed chicken remains grinding under the big man's heel. The raccoon lumbered a few steps and hissed loudly. Bill focused on the raccoon, and I took my chance.

I tucked a wide-eyed Ernie under one arm and carried him like a long, shaggy football. I charged up my stairs. Below me a car nosed down the alley and the raccoon charged. The masked man turned and ran.

I squinted. There was some kind of design on the man's jacket, but he disappeared before I got a good look.

The raccoon's ringed tail slid under my stairs and disappeared as high beams filled the narrow space with light.

With shaking hands, I shoved the key into my lock. I hesitated and looked down again. The headlights flicked off and, in the dim glow from my bug light, I caught a glimpse of the figure behind the sedan's wheel — the pony-tailed man.

I wrenched my door open, and Ernie and I were inside my apartment. I bolted the door and leaned against it. After a few minutes I blew out a breath and put Ernie on the floor. My thudding heart slowed. I peeked out the window — no sign of man, car, or territorial raccoon.

I pulled the curtain closed and made myself walk away from it. It was one a.m. Ben would still be at Walter's or out looking for him.

After the snort incident, I didn't want to come across as some wimpy chick who ran to her almost boyfriend every time something scared her. I was an auxiliary deputy, for pity's sake! With training I could be a real deputy someday, if they'd let me wear my own shoes.

I rubbed my hands across my face. I was safe. My doors had deadbolts. I peeked into the alley again. Empty.

I'd tell Ben about this in the morning in a professional, nonchalant, semi-law enforcement manner. Unofficial, of course. He'd be impressed.

I looked down at Ernie. "We're tough. Nobody intimidates us. Right?"

Ernie's eyes met mine. He squatted and whizzed out a big yellow puddle on my living room rug.

I sopped up the tinkle with paper towels, doused the rug with cleaning solution, and closed all my remaining blinds.

I shed my smelly clothes and ended the evening by moving around the apartment in my pink cowgirl pajamas, Ernie tight at my heels like a nervous, wiener-shaped shadow. I stacked soup cans mounded with piles of spare change by my front door, then did the same with the door in the kitchen. I doublechecked both deadbolts.

Then I locked all my windows. If some jerk wanted to crawl up a ladder and break glass, he'd be dealing with one alerted woman. One alerted, armed woman.

I tucked my biggest butcher knife under my pillow and patted the bed. Ernie leapt up and burrowed in next to me. He pressed his short legs straight out, stretched his paws, and nestled in tight. Then we both stared at the chair wedged under the bedroom doorknob until we fell asleep.

TEN

The next morning, I half-dozed in the dim light of my bedroom while nightmare images of a crazed Bill Clinton gnawed at the edges of my consciousness. I'd just unwrapped my cramped fingers from the knife's hilt when soup cans and coins clattered to the wood floor of my living room. I jerked upright, fully awake. I snatched up the knife and squinted. Ernie yapped as ferociously as a small dog could while backing his hind-end into his owner's stomach. I climbed out of bed and opened my door a crack.

"It's me!" Kitty trilled. "I brought Patrice, too."

A soup can rolled to my toes. I stepped over it.

"Jeeze, I forgot you were coming," I said.

Ernie flew past me, every part of his body wriggling. In that way only little dogs can do, he threw back his head and cockadoodle-dooed with morning joy.

I squinted at Kitty. Under her red cardigan sweater she sported a "Dog the Bounty Hunter" T-shirt. Her knobby knees poked out from beneath red Lycra bicycle shorts.

"I'm afraid to ask about that outfit," I said.

Kitty scooped Ernie into her arms, and he licked her chin. "Nancy Schnebbly posted a reward for capturing Walter. I read it in the *Eavesdropper*." She leaned forward. "I'm planning to bring him in and maybe collect the cash — right after I break up with the nincompoop."

"Weiner-dude!" Patrice followed Kitty into the room and scratched Ernie behind his wispy ears.

Since the bank robbery yesterday, she'd sliced through her jet black hair with bright burgundy streaks. Either that, or she'd sustained a major arterial scalp wound.

I needed coffee. I shuffled to the kitchen and tossed my knife on the table. Patrice plunked her backpack next to it.

Patrice fingered her new eyebrow rings, then pointed at the knife. "What's with the *Psycho* prop?"

Kitty stepped over a Campbell's Cream of Mushroom can. "Does this have something to do with the murder and the bank robbery?" She looked around at the drawn blinds and soup cans. "Do you need some hot cocoa or a martini or something? Should I call my therapist?"

"No, I'm fine." I loaded the coffee maker, then gathered up the rolling cans.

"Patrice wants to work on the lighting," Kitty said. "She thinks it's giving the illusion that I'm . . . old. Then I'm off to find Walter."

I slid a cup of coffee across my yellow fifties tabletop. "Kitty, maybe you should hold off on looking for Walter. He's sort of on a rampage." I took a sip of my own coffee. "And like you said, he might have killed Fred. At the very least he's involved." I poured Patrice a coffee and handed it to her. "Aren't you working today?"

"The bank's closed," Patrice said. "They're in mourning or something. Sorry I couldn't wait on you guys yesterday. I feel awful."

"It's not your fault," I said.

"If Rhonda'd been on time, I could've made your deposit before that whole thing with the geezer went down," Patrice said. "Then you would have been covered by the bank's insurance."

I poured a scoop of kibbles into Ernie's dish. He simultaneously growled and wagged his tail, then stuck his face in his bowl.

"Who's Rhonda? Another teller?"

"Yep," Patrice said. "She was like, an hour late yesterday."

"Patrice is going to help me bounty hunt." Kitty patted Patrice's puffy flowered sleeve. "We're going to check out Fred and Walter and snoop into their criminal records, spending habits, and whatnot. We're hacking into Webster's. We'll probably dig up oodles of dirt."

"Web . . ." I said. "It's the Web."

"Huh?"

"Never mind."

Patrice pulled her laptop from her backpack and popped it open. I scanned her outfit — typical tongue stud, and various loops and rings dangled from her face. She wore super-low-rider jeans and clunky Doc Marten boots. I bent close and eyed the sweet black T-shirt with the feminine sleeves and delicate white flowers. The center of each blossom proved to be a tiny, grinning skull. Somehow, I felt better.

"All that information can't be legal." I glanced at Patrice's screen.

"It is . . . mostly. You can find out a ton without hacking." Patrice hit a few keys. "Hacking's a lot more fun. Like, stimulating, you know?" She pointed at the screen. "Cool. Fred's in debt up to his eyeballs."

I escaped to my room where I slipped into jeans, a black sweater, and my Jimmy Choos. I scooped my smelly, still damp beer and sauerkraut-laden clothes from the floor and carried the bundle to the kitchen where I shoved it into the stackable washer-dryer.

"I'm going to pay Nancy Schnebbly a visit." I loaded soap and twisted the knob.

"Oh good!" Kitty pressed her palms together and wiggled her fingers. "We're a family of bounty hunters," she pulled her baggy shirt out from her belly and looked down at it, "like 'Dog' and his crew."

"Kitty, we're not bounty hunters." I caught a wriggling, freshly fed Ernie and clipped his leash to his harness. "I'm just doing some checking for Ben." I put on what I hoped was a stern face and wiggled my leash handle at Patrice. "And you shouldn't hack!"

Patrice grabbed Ernie's leash and stood up. "I'll walk the little weiner-dude. You go investigate."

ELEVEN

I stopped at the flower shop on the outskirts of town and charged a cheap fern. I jabbed in a plastic stake and stuck a free sympathy card on it, then picked up a to-go coffee from the drive thru across the street. I drove to 25 Dunes View and stared at the giant hills of sand beside the expensive development. I swiped on another layer of mascara for courage. Next stop, my old nemesis, Nancy von Dickel-Schnebbly.

I took a deep breath and blew it out. Those panties were ancient history. Getting our money back and finding Fred's killer was what mattered now.

I climbed out of the car, marched up the cobblestone path, and pressed the bell.

A petite woman answered the door, dressed head-to-toe in black — not widow's garb, but an exercise tank and yoga pants. I could see the seventh-grade Nancy in her face. Her hooked nose and beady eyes still looked like she ought to be laying eggs somewhere on a tree branch.

"Yes?"

"I, uh . . ." I fidgeted from one foot to the other.

She peered at me and blinked her bright eyes several times. "Kate?" She hopped forward and looked me up and down. "Kate London! I heard you were back from Chicago."

"My condolences," I said. I shoved the plant at her chest. "I found your husband's body yesterday." I hesitated. "I'm really sorry."

She took the plant and placed it on her hall table, then ruffled a hand through her short brown hair. "Thank you . . . I guess. We were getting a divorce."

I nodded. "Been there."

We both fell silent. I waited for her to invite me in. She didn't move.

I opened my mouth expecting one of my custom-designed, semi-law enforcement, unofficial-but-with-excellent-footwear questions.

Instead, this popped out: "Pumpkin butt."

Nancy's eyebrows shot up, and she took a step back. "Pardon me?"

My own brows scrunched down, and I gritted my teeth. My voice hissed out through them. "Pumpkin butt. That's what they called me all through junior high."

"Is that what this is about?" Nancy cocked her head and blinked some more. "My future former husband's dead, and you came all the way out here to bust my chops over something that happened in seventh grade?"

"You stole from me! From my gym locker! You're —" I punched my hands into my hips and cocked my head. "You're a panty thief! Do you have any idea how humiliating that was? Watching you auction off my underwear? And my very worst pair, too! With the Halloween pumpkins on them. In *April!*"

Nancy reddened, then puffed up her chest and lifted her scrawny neck.

"It was funny," she said. "Heck, it probably boosted your popularity. Mine skyrocketed . . . for a while."

Mine had, too. I scowled at her anyway. "It was a scuzzy thing to do."

"Hello? Two decades ago . . . ? It was just underpants, for God's sake. Don't be such a sorehead. Time to get over it." She grabbed her jacket and purse and sidled past me. "I'm in a hurry."

I looked at her feet. "Oh. My God! Are those the new Michael Kors sandals?"

She didn't even glance down. "Uh-huh."

I sighed at the beautiful blue leather and tried to regroup.

"Do you know what's going on with your uncle?" I followed her down the path. "Has he been getting senile or something?"

"It's Fred who was getting senile." She looked at her watch. "Look, I have a meeting and a work-out class. I can't keep all these people waiting."

"What do you mean Fred was getting senile?"

"We were over a long time ago — the bimbo from the bank — the teller? I understood that. But . . . everything else . . ." She flapped her hand in the air, then used it to open the door to a big white SUV. She climbed in and rolled the window down.

"What bimbo from the bank?" I stood at her window. "What everything else?"

"Look, just — stuff, okay? I'm late here." She started the engine.

"Somebody ransacked your uncle's apartment," I said. "Whatever they're looking for, they think I have it. I've been robbed, threatened, locked in a tiny kitchen with —" I caught myself. "My aunt's running around in a 'Dog the Bounty Hunter' T-shirt, for cripes' sake!"

"Your aunt." She smiled. The smile faded,

and she looked out at the choppy waters of the lake. "I think my uncle's in trouble, okay?"

"I'll say he's in trouble," I said. "He'd better hope the sheriff catches him before I do."

"That's not what I mean." Her jaw clenched, and she looked out at the water again. "Look, find my uncle before he gets hurt, the reward's five grand. I'll see that and raise you five grand donated straight to the Egyptian."

She frowned again and waited.

Ten grand. I did some quick mental calculations and by the time the numbers registered, I had it spent. "I'll want to ask you some more questions."

"I've got to go. Come to the Fitness Frenzy in an hour or so. I've got a meeting to figure out what to do about . . . about . . . Fred, right now, then we'll talk."

I nodded and turned toward my car.

"Kate?"

I faced her.

"Do you know why I did it?" she said

Did she kill Fred? My breath caught in my throat. "Did what?"

"Took your underpants." She looked down at her steering wheel, then met my eyes. "I was always so jealous of you. Everywhere we went, you came first. I was the nerdy friend — like-like . . . afterbirth or something."

I squirmed. I'd forgotten how weird Nancy could be.

"Nerdy? We were both nerdy," I said. "I was the biggest nerd on the planet."

"Not true. You lived with your glamorous aunt." She looked into the distance. "You went exciting places like Hollywood, Las Vegas, Milwaukee. You were so . . . *pretty.*"

"Me? Pretty?" I straightened, sucked in my gut, and patted my disobedient curls.

She reached out and touched my hand. "I'm not sure what's going on, but I have a theory."

I watched her brake lights as she exited the complex's private road. She knew something. And she was willing to tell.

I slid behind the wheel, took a sip of cold coffee, and dug for my grocery list. I scrawled a few notes and got to "bank bimbo." Patrice might be a lot of things, a bimbo she was not. I pulled out my cell and punched her number.

"Oh. The bimbo? That's easy!" She read me Rhonda Wollenberg's address.

Twelve

Back in Mudd Lake, I parked my Riviera in front of a shabby duplex and knocked on Rhonda's door.

After a few long minutes and repeated knocks, she answered. From the tangles in her big eighties-flashback hair, I must have woken her. She wore a long pink terrycloth robe and nothing else.

"Can I come in?" I'd planned what to say again, something clever and scripted and tuned in to just the right station to get me inside. When I opened my mouth, my cable went out. I eased my foot forward in case she slammed the door. "I'd like to talk to you."

She squinted at me through puffy eyes. "Aren't you from the theatre?"

Unofficial, Ben had said.

I switched my mental channels and tried again. "The theatre, uh-huh." I nodded. "The Egyptian."

"You guys are doing *Little Shop of Horrors,* right? I played Ronnette in high school. Get it? Rhonda, the Ronnette!" She opened her puffy eyes wide and broke into the opening bars of the first number, "Little shop, little shop of horrors!"

I grimaced at her off-key, nasal twang. I caught myself and stretched my face into a broad grin. "Gre-e-eat! That was great!"

She gave a little bow. "Are you collecting or something? I'm really busy and kind of broke right now, but thanks." She made a move to shut the door.

"Um, no. That's not why I'm here. I, uh, found Fred Schnebbly's body," I said.

She froze and stared at me.

"At Walter's." I still had my foot in the door. "Can I talk to you about him?"

She looked past me to the street. "No. I don't think so." She pushed the door toward my foot.

I looked down at my glove-leather Jimmy Choo. "Hey, don't scrape the leather!" I yanked my boot back and poked my head out instead.

Rhonda trapped my cheekbones in her door jam.

"Please," I said, "I know you and Fred were . . . um, close." My head was locked in place, so I slid my eyes to her.

"Yeah . . ." She met my gaze, hesitated. "We were."

I waited, watched her. I didn't have much choice. My head remained pinned.

Finally, she let go of the door and motioned me to follow her. We wove between big boxes littered across the living room floor.

I rubbed my cheeks, then pointed to the cardboard cartons. "Are you moving?"

"I'm going to have to." Rhonda snatched a pack of Virginia Slims off the threadbare arm of her recliner and shook one loose. After lighting it, she flopped into the chair and pointed to the couch.

I shifted a shiny vinyl handbag the approximate weight and shape of a cinderblock and sat down.

"I'm out of here, before I get evicted." She exhaled blue smoke. "I can't make my rent."

"The bank'll be reopening in a day or so," I said. "Won't they keep you on?"

"I doubt it. Not with Nancy Schnebbly running things. Anyway, I can't afford rent and these, too." She whipped open her bathrobe and held the chenille lapels wide.

"What — ?" I blinked a few times like a possum caught in the glare of a Mack truck's high beams. I'd never seen a boob job up close. I ripped my eyes back to Rhonda's face and tried to look casual. I focused on the cigarette dangling from her lip while a blush climbed my neck and spread to my cheeks. It burnt like a heat lamp under my skin. "They're uh —"

"I know. Big." She tugged her robe together. "Anyway, the surgery bill's past due."

"They can't repossess·those." I furrowed my brow. "Can they?"

"No, but they can sue me. And they might not fix their mistake." She pulled her robe apart again. "Did you notice my nipple problem?"

I fought back a wince.

"I think it's real obvious." She looked down and pointed first at one breast, then the other.

I swallowed hard and pretended I was looking at something inanimate, a light fixture — maybe two light fixtures.

"See how they aim in opposite directions? I've gotta get that redone." Rhonda pulled her robe together again and tightened the belt.

She jabbed her cigarette at the wall, pointing it in the same direction as her left nipple. A framed picture of Fred Schnebbly in his red bow tie and wire-rimmed glasses sat on the table.

"Fred was supposed to pay off my boob bill yesterday. Now, because of this tragedy, I've got to move in with my brother out by the mall. That way I can start installments with the BYOB."

"BYOB?" I said.

"Yeah, Be You Only Better, the surgery joint."

"I'm sorry about Fred," I said.

She sighed. "Poor guy." She shook her head and took another drag on her cigarette. "Walter killing his own nephew. Who would have thought?"

"Nephew by marriage, and I'm not sure he did it." I watched her for a reaction. "I saw three other men at the crime scene."

Her blue eyes stared through me. "Did you? Hunh . . ." She stubbed out her cigarette, stood, and crossed to the window. "Fred's had his share of troubles lately. I thought these boobs would cheer him up."

"What kind of troubles?"

She kept her back to me and shook her head. "The poor guy . . ." she repeated, her voice low. She turned toward me and rolled her hand in the air, her voice back to its regular, nasal pitch. "Oh, you know. The divorce. The usual."

"Can you tell me why you were late,

yesterday?" I shifted forward in my seat. "The police will want to know."

"Well, then they can ask me." She crossed her arms below her paranormal chest. "You're not a cop, are you?"

I hesitated. "Not exactly."

"Okay then, Not Exactly, I gotta get back to my packing." She walked to the table and pulled another cigarette from the pack. "You can see yourself out."

She sat and crossed her legs. I stared at her shin. On it rose a red tattoo of a woman sporting horns and a long forked tail. The devil-woman hoisted a pair of appropriately oversized pom-poms.

Thirteen

I skirted the Sausage Festival and cut over to the Fitness Frenzy. I parked, pulled out my grocery pad, and added to my list. Under Rhonda's name I wrote *affair, Fred had troubles, boob job debt,* and finally *alibi?*

I slurped a mouthful of cold coffee and grimaced, then I dropped my pen and snorted the bitter liquid up my nostrils. Several doors down, a gray sedan had parked. Behind the wheel sat the pony-tailed man.

"God, he's everywhere," I muttered. I blew my nose on a paper napkin.

Heart thudding, I scribbled the sedan's number on my pad. The man climbed out of the car and crossed to the muddy flower-bed in front of the gym's picture window. While he looked inside, I reached over the back seat and grabbed Ernie's blanket. I wrapped it over my hair and forehead, then dug in the glove box and found a pair of

Kitty's old sunglasses: black, encrusted with rhinestones. I slipped them on and pulled the blanket across my nose and mouth. I tucked it over my shoulder and took shallow breaths around the dog hair. I glanced in the rearview. I looked like a chilly and slightly demented Muslim movie star, but it would have to do. I didn't know if the pony-tailed man would recognize me, but I couldn't take the risk.

I hopped out, palmed my cell, and speed-dialed Ben while I headed down the block.

"Boy, someone really tore Walter's place apart last night," Ben said. He paused. "You sound all muffled."

"I'm disguised," I told him. "The pony-tailed man from the bank — from everywhere — he's here — at the fitness center on fourth street. He followed Nancy." Fibers stuck to my lip gloss. I made a *puhh* sound, spitting them back into the humid fabric.

I'd reached the sidewalk near the entrance. The pony-tailed man turned from the front window and watched me.

I looked away and babbled the only Middle Eastern words I knew. "So. Falafels . . . tabooleh, babba ganoush. Uh-huh. Shish kabob."

The man climbed the brick step and

entered the building. I hissed into the phone. "Ben, the pony-tailed man, he's watching Nancy. I think he might be after her."

"You've got to be kidding me." Ben finally understood.

I described the gray sedan and told Ben I'd meet him inside the building.

"I'm a minute or two away. Don't do anything until I get there," he said.

I hung up and stepped into the deserted lobby.

I found the black plastic events sign. Only one exercise class, and it sounded like a Starbucks special: *Yoga-Latties! A unique Yoga-Pilates Blend: First Floor, Room Four.*

"Don't do anything," Ben had said. I stood in front of Room Four and wondered what "anything" meant. It was nebulous. Kind of like "unofficial."

I eased the door open.

Rows of women stretched while standing on individual exercise mats. Nancy von Dickel-Schnebbly stood at the far end of the room. Behind her hung a black floor to ceiling net. The net held maybe thirty giant round blue exercise balls. They shifted and rolled against each other.

I looked for the source of the movement. My eyebrows shot up under my veil. To the

109

side stood Kitty. She gripped a rope that hung from the netting.

"I've taken lots of Yoga, see? I've got excellent balance." Kitty wobbled on one skinny leg like a geriatric stork.

Nancy took a step toward her. "Maybe you should let go of that —"

"Woops!" Kitty listed to the left and capsized. In an effort to right herself, she tugged the rope.

The entire net released on one side and slipped away from the wall, exposing all its big globes at once like an overexcited stripper. The balls trembled, suspended in space.

"There," Kitty straightened and bent one leg in the air. "I just needed to focus. I had a guru once who —" She looked up. "Uh-oh."

"Get out of the way!"

"Timber!"

The entire towering, wobbling mass collapsed into bouncing, rolling chaos. Shouting filled the room. Women scrambled across the floor.

Kitty dodged a giant sphere and flattened herself against the wall. Next to her, Nancy did the same. Women crouched and covered their heads while they scooted between the bounding balls. Everyone plastered themselves around the perimeter of the room.

110

I zigzagged across the floor, dodging globes as I went. One rolled against my head and knocked my sunglasses to the floor. I bent to scoop them up, and when I got to my feet, Kitty was standing by herself. I waded knee-deep through the transparent blue orbs and reached her.

"The pony-tailed man." I straightened the rhinestone glasses on my nose. "He's here."

"Your boyfriend's here, too." Kitty pointed to the doorway. "Since when did you convert to Islam?"

"He's not exactly my boyfr—" My eyes swept to the entrance.

Ben leaned against the doorframe, arms folded across his chest. His tan uniform pants accented narrow hips and lanky legs. He looked at me and shook his head. His lip curved up enough that his dimple appeared. He waded toward us. I tugged the dog blanket off my head and draped it over my arm.

One of the women looked Ben up and down and caught her breath.

"Wow," another whispered. "No wonder we vote for him."

Ben reached us. He leaned over and brushed my hair out of my eyes. All the strands flew toward his palm. He moved his hand, and my hair moved with it.

111

"You might need a new cream rinse," Ben said.

"Static electricity," I said. "Must be from all the friction."

Ben raised an eyebrow, grinned that lopsided smile, and his eyes sparkled.

My heart skipped a beat, and I took two steps back. Most of my hair settled down, but the rest of me did not. I was very aware of Ben standing there, grinning and giving off heat.

I tried to focus and scanned the crowd. Everybody seemed okay. A few women pushed balls at each other or kicked them in the air.

"Did you find the pony-tailed man?" I said.

"No, but I checked around outside," Ben said. "The car you described is gone."

One of the women from the class interrupted us. "Excuse me, but in all this pandemonium, our teacher seems to have disappeared."

FOURTEEN

An exit door across from us stood open a crack. Several Yoga-Latties participants agreed, Nancy had left through it while the balls had been flying. On the other side of the door, a hallway led to the back of the building and an exit.

Ben interviewed women inside the building, while Kitty and I stood out front amid milling ladies in various exercise get-ups.

"I thought you were doing lighting today," I said.

"Oh, we moved through that pretty quick," Kitty said. "We're going to use the purple footlights and the fog machine — again. Patrice thinks we need a lot of fog. All our sets are so foggy, lately."

"We're atmospheric," I said.

"Anyway, I'm on a tight schedule today with the bounty-hunting business and whatnot." Kitty looked at her watch.

"I'm guessing you didn't just wake up

with the urge to Yoga-Lattie," I said.

"Patrice dug up the poop on Nancy, the divorce filing and whatnot, and we found out that she taught over here." Kitty lowered her voice. "I know you two had some sort of falling out way back when, and you seemed so nervous with the soup cans and knife and so forth, I figured you might need help with your part of the investigating." Kitty wiggled her arms and legs. "My balance is usually so fabulous. I bet it's that darned Mercury."

I kept Nancy's offer of the additional reward to myself. "Like I said before, maybe bounty-hunting isn't the best idea."

"Don't be silly." Kitty tugged at her T-shirt, straightening *Dog the Bounty Hunter*'s grizzled jaw line. "I've got tons of experience with this sort of thing. *Mayhem in Manhattan* and *Dastardly Dames* were both detective movies, you know."

Ben trotted down the steps. "There's no sign of Nancy Schnebbly." He pointed to her SUV. "Her car's still here. A few folks saw a pony-tailed man in the hallway. And somebody said they saw Bill Clinton. Nancy must've slipped out during the commotion — and she never came back." Ben held out Nancy's Michael Kors sandals with one surgically gloved hand. "She took her purse, but she left these."

I caught my breath and stared at the strappy blue beauties dangling from his fingers. "She didn't leave on her own," I said.

"You bet your noodles she didn't," Kitty said. "Those are the real thing. Look at that heel — gorgeous."

Ben looked at her. "So?"

Another woman stepped closer and eyed the shoes. "I've seen these at Imelda's Closet. No markdowns on them yet." She reached out a finger to touch a strap. "Nancy told me they cost her six hundred samoles."

We all nodded.

"As in dollars?" Ben stared as if the shoes had arrived by meteor.

Just then Verna puttered to the curb in her lemon yellow Volkswagen. She rolled her window down. "Yoo-hoo."

Kitty waved.

"Verna and I are grabbing lunch at the mall," Kitty said to me. "Rehearsal's at three-thirty. We called it special — just so you can learn the Audrey Two. Don't be late!"

My stomach wrapped itself into a tightly twisted knot. I hiccupped.

Kitty climbed into the passenger seat of

the little bug, and they chugged off.

Ben and I walked around the block to the festival. We stood at a tiny table in front of a giant plastic hotdog.

"So, he shows up at two crime scenes in as many days." Ben sipped his coke. "A bank robbery and a murder. Now this. Who the heck is this guy?"

"Wait, I have his plate number." I dug in my purse and got my grocery list.

Ben pressed a button on the radio clipped to his shoulder and read the license number into it. He hooked his sunglasses in his shirt and skimmed my notes. I filled him in on my visits with Rhonda and Nancy.

I swallowed a bite of chili-and-onion-laden Coney dog. "I should probably mention this, too: some guy, um, kind of threatened me last night. And the pony-tailed man was there, too. Right after."

Ben listened, and his blue-gray eyes turned serious. "I don't like this. Anything else happens, you call me right away. Meanwhile, the state police have this guy's description, and anybody caught with a Bill Clinton mask gets hauled in for questioning. I'll issue a 'be on the lookout' for Nancy, although I don't think I can officially call it an abduction."

Ben's radio beeped. He stepped out of

range of the curious hotdog vendor.

Ben clicked off and came back to the table. "Are you sure you got that plate number right?"

"Yes. I'm positive," I said.

"They're not seeing that license number in the state information database," Ben said.

"Is that unusual?" I kept my voice low.

"I guess it could be new." Ben scanned my notes again.

I remembered the plate's condition and shook my head. "Not with that much rust."

Ben shifted his muscular shoulders and pulled me away from a gaggle of women that had inched closer from their nearby table. Mudd Lake's recent crime wave coupled with rumors that Ben and I were "an item" had the town's gossip antennae at full extension.

"I once saw a fake license in a seminar," Ben whispered. "They made it by cutting two plates in half then soldering the partials together."

I pictured that. "Sounds pretty sophisticated."

Ben nodded and put a hand on my shoulder. His eyes turned that serious steely gray. "It belonged to a professional hit-man."

I swallowed hard.

"Look, you need to be careful, just do

your rehearsal and forget about all this." Ben looked at his watch. "I've got a class on wax denture impressions at 1:00. I'm coming over right after to get a formal report about last night." Ben hooked a finger in one of my curls and searched my eyes. "Be *very* careful, okay?"

I nodded. My breath came faster. I scanned the streets for any sign of the pony-tailed man while we walked back to our cars.

FIFTEEN

I drove the long way to skirt the festival traffic and parked in front of the Egyptian. I found Patrice in the light booth at the back of the auditorium.

She flipped a switch and green strobes flashed across the snoozing Audrey Two, giving her a menacing look.

She looked up. "Hey, did you have something funny in your pocket? I was going to put your clothes in the dryer, but your jeans have a big pink spot on them."

"What?" I looked at her puzzled, and then I remembered. I gasped. The only thing in my pocket was the bill Walter gave me last night — the twenty dollar bill. ·

"Come on!" I grabbed her arm and pulled her down the aisle.

"I probably shouldn't have mentioned it. I know you have bigger problems." Patrice followed me through the theatre to the back stairs. "But I thought you'd want to know."

In my kitchen, my jeans lay across the top of the counter, still wet. A large fuschia spot covered the right front pocket.

Patrice looked over my shoulder. "Those jeans are toast."

I slipped my hand into the damp fabric and caught the soggy bill between two fingers. I slid it out. The once green bill almost glowed with a hot magenta tint.

"Whoa. I've never seen a counterfeit bill before." Patrice reached a stubby eggplant-colored nail forward and turned the damp paper over. "Or wait." She peered at the bill. "That's like what they trained us on at the bank."

"What do you mean?"

Patrice pointed to the shadowy picture of Abraham Lincoln off to one side. "See this? Not counting the way-funky color scheme they've got going here, this dude's the wrong dead president."

I squinted at the bill.

Patrice aimed her finger at Ulysses S. Grant's stern face in the center, then at Abe Lincoln's smaller, but equally stern face, barely visible at the side.

"They should match," Patrice said.

"I'm calling Ben," I said. I pulled out my cell and punched Ben's speed-dial.

His voicemail went off — probably still in

class. I left a message for him to come straight to the theatre, to cut out early if he could.

"Yapyapyapyapyap!" Ernie flew through the kitchen, skidded his toenails across my hardwood living room floor, and leapt at the sidelight window.

I got there in time to see a man with a shaved scalp climb off the bottom rung of my stairs and into the alley. He looked up. A rubber Bill Clinton mask dangled from his fingertips. He saw me in the window, ducked, and struggled to yank the mask over his head. He tugged at it a few seconds, ripped it off, and mouthed some swear-words. He stuffed the mask in his jacket pocket and stalked down the alley.

I stared at his back as he strode away. A scary-looking snake tattoo crawled from his denim collar up the back of his shaved skull, and a brightly colored insignia filled his denim jacket: a familiar cheesy red woman with a forked tail and horns hefting two big pom-poms. Underneath I read the words "Devil's Cheerleaders."

I speed-walked through the apartment and clipped Ernie's leash to his harness. I shoved the damp twenty in an envelope and stuffed it in my purse. Hoisting the strap over my shoulder, I yanked open the kitchen door.

"Let's get out of here, Patrice." I tugged her into the back stairwell, and we ran down to the theatre, with Ernie leading the way.

I slid my grocery pad out of my bag. I ripped off a page and scrawled Rhonda Wollenberg's name followed by Fred's, then "Devil's Cheerleaders."

"Hack into Fort Knox if you want. Just find out everything you can on these people," I said.

She looked at the list.

"The Cheerleaders, huh? I don't need to go online to tell you they're mean, and they like to party. You can find them every Tuesday night at Zero's out on the highway. Bike Night."

I handed her Ernie's leash and dropped my purse on the seat next to her. "Do not take your eyes off this bag."

"No problem," Patrice flipped open her computer. "Me and Weiner-dude — we're on the case."

She patted the seat, and Ernie hopped up and tucked himself into a tight ball in front of my purse. Patrice brought the lights up on the stage as I headed toward it. I stopped and thought about my options.

The bill was fake, the guy in the alley

looked menacing, and Rhonda's tattoo matched the guy's denim jacket. I could call the state police, but other than the bill what did I really have? The mask thing was iffy at best. And if the pink twenty-dollar bill turned out to be the key to the crime spree, and Albert Schwenck learned that a big case development happened while Ben was off making denture molds, then what?

Ben said he'd be here right after class. I took a deep breath and blew it out. This could wait an hour or so.

I walked down the aisle.

A dozen or so members of the *Little Shop* cast milled around on stage.

"Do you think she can do it?" A willowy black high school girl named Mary, who played one of the three doo-wop singers, stood center stage and eyed the Audrey Two. The other two singers, frizzy-haired redheaded twins, worked out a dance step.

The one on the left finished her move and said, "The *CracklePops* Foundation. I thought they only funded, you know," she lowered her voice, "stuff that's good."

I straightened my shoulders and marched up onto the stage.

Kitty looked at me and smiled encouragingly. I read fear in her eyes.

"Oh, this will be outstanding. I can just

feel it." She patted my shoulder.

"We'll just block today," Verna said. "So that Kate will get a feel for the movement."

I stared at the big Audrey Two puppet. "Block?" I knew I should know what block meant, but I drew a blank.

Kitty whispered, "Blocking means move from one mark to the other around the stage."

I nodded. "No problem."

"We stuck special green tape on all your marks." Kitty pointed to the boards. "So they'd stand out."

My heart skipped a beat, then kicked up a notch. It bounced against my ribcage while I pulled the felt curtain apart on the back of Audrey Two's cranium. I inspected the dark, fuzzy insides. A secretarial chair, a few levers to work the jaws, and extension rods to make the puppet appear to grow tall, it looked simple enough. I hiccupped.

"Just do your best, kiddo." Kitty leaned close and held her script to shield us from the cast. "We'll keep it short," she whispered. "Just raise everybody's confidence level."

"Let's go, people," Verna called out. "Let's have Kate get in and move around. The prop man will run the smaller puppet, and we'll skip the dancing root entirely."

"Okay." I huffed up a breath for courage. "I'm going in."

I hunched down and crawled through the four-foot fabric opening. I slid into the secretarial chair and peered through the mesh at the murky looking stage. Inside my dark felt pod, I inhaled dank air tinged with stale body odor. I sneezed and followed it with a hiccup.

"Okay, Kate, give it a try," Verna said. "Move to your next mark."

I guessed and rolled to the next spot but missed it and ended up on pink tape. I squinted at the tiny square of stage visible below my feet.

"Sorry, I can't see too well," I said. I hiccupped.

I slid my chair left, and the Audrey glided across the floor faster than I expected. I knocked into something and swiveled sideways.

"Woopsy!"

I peered through the black mesh screen in Audrey's eyeball and watched a blurry Verna catch the plywood florist counter.

I concentrated, remembered to breathe, and tried again. Green tape. A little better.

A counterfeit bill — what did that have to do with Fred's death, Nancy's possible disappearance, and Walter's shenanigans?

And a bad counterfeit bill at that.

I heard Verna's muffled voice. "Try it again, dear."

I slid a few feet, and something stopped me. I tried moving.

Whack!

I swiveled and pressed my face to Audrey's eyeball. A flat lay toppled on its back on the stage.

"Was that me?" I said. "Sorry . . ."

"I'll get it," a voice said.

I heard disgruntled mumbling.

"Kate seems to have a visibility problem," Verna said.

I scooted back and forth in the chair and concentrated on not getting dizzy. I pulled the bars that hung suspended over my head. The Audrey Two's mouth opened wide, and cool air washed over me. I opened the jaws and snapped them a few more times.

What about Nancy? Had she run? Or had the pony-tailed man and Bill Clinton taken her? And why was Bill Clinton — that guy with the tattoo on his head — after me? What did he want?

I scooted my chair along and used my knees to move the Styrofoam flower pot around my legs.

Nancy must have been kidnapped. Only a professional hit man could make me walk away from those Michael Kors sandals.

I lifted off my seat and gripped the rods beside me to extend Audrey's head up. I locked them in place and leaned forward, tipping the Audrey to face the actors. Something jostled me as I banged into the set again and knocked myself backward.

"Crap!" I plopped down hard on the chair and let the rods slide back down.

Kitty poked her head through the fabric behind me. "Try to be a little more careful. You're upsetting the cast."

My stomach sank. Opening night loomed four nights away.

I shoved away images of devil women tattoos. I called through the little hole in Audrey's mouth, "Should we try a number?"

"Okay," Verna said. I heard the doubt in her voice and watched her shadowy form cross to the piano. "Ready, Scotty?"

I heard Scotty Forsythe's deep baritone voice and the strains to "Sominex/Suppertime."

I squinted at the dim marks under me. I scooted my chair and dragged my flower pot. I looked down again and peered at the tape. I'd hit a green mark.

Cool.

I tried standing to tip Audrey's head

down. I concentrated and tried to copy the way I'd seen Leo do it.

The puppet rocked forward, and I lost my balance. I overcompensated and pulled sideways. My flowerpot and chair went over and took me with it. I felt my feet lift off the floor.

"Kate, watch it!" Kitty squawked.

"Help!" The thing was top heavy. I wobbled and yanked at the handles inside, but I was off balance. I couldn't stop it.

"Hey!" a female voice yelled.

Something broke my fall just for a second, then I went over on my side.

"Aaaack!"

Then a crash.

The music stopped.

A cry of pain, then gasps.

"Oh God." I squirmed out of the capsized puppet and shoved my chair out of the way.

The willowy black singer from the chorus, Mary, lay sprawled under a wall from Mushnik's flower shop.

"Oh my gosh. Are you okay?" I got up and leaned over her.

"Get away, you!" She scooted from under the flat and wiggled her legs. "You — you menace!"

"I don't think anything's broken, dear." Verna fanned at Mary with her script.

"Scotty!"

Scotty, a former ER doctor, jogged across the stage. He leaned his cottony white head over the girl and felt her legs. He bent both her knees and rotated her ankles. "You'll be all right, Mary. Just got the wind knocked out of you, I suspect."

"I'm not working with her," the guy who played Seymour, jabbed a finger in my direction. "She's gonna kill somebody."

"Yeah," said one of the frizzy redheads. "She's dangerous."

Disgruntled mumbles filled the stage.

"Mary, I am so sorry!" I said. My heart pounded. The lights glared overhead. I hiccupped.

Mary scrambled to her feet. She towered over my five-foot-six frame.

"I'm only here for extra credit at school." She shoved her script into my chest. "It's not worth it. I'm taking marching band instead."

She stomped off the stage.

Seymour moaned.

"Let's call it a day, folks," Verna said.

"Look, I'll practice, I'll . . . I'll manage . . . somehow. I — I promise!" I said.

I yanked Audrey upright, plopped on my chair, and scooted inside to hide.

A murky but familiar shape appeared by

the orchestra pit. My engine gave a little purr.

"Ben!" I scrambled out of the puppet and bounded down the steps. I called over my shoulder, "I'll practice, you guys. You'll see! I've got to talk to Ben."

Sixteen

While Verna worked to reassure the cast, I motioned for Patrice to come down the aisle with my purse.

"No worries here!" Kitty said. "Kate will be stellar, you'll see!" She trotted behind us to the greenroom.

Ben shook his head. "Walter robbed three party stores out on the highway this afternoon. I'm thinking of ordering a shoot on sight."

"Did you find something good?" Kitty wanted to know.

I sat down on the greenroom's old leather couch and put the pink bill on the table between us. "Look at this."

"Wow. Where'd that come from?" Ben stared at the twenty.

"Is that the new currency?" Kitty bent over the table. "That color is far better than the Canadian pink, quite eye-catching."

"Walter stuck this in my hand before he

knocked me down at the festival. I wonder if this is what those guys were after at the apartment," I said. "And that guy in the mask in the alley last night."

"And today," Patrice said.

"Bill Clinton came here?" Kitty's eyes grew wide. "No wonder you were nervous."

"Today, huh?" Ben raised an eyebrow and looked at me. "We need to talk." He lifted the soggy bill up with two fingers. "What happened to this?"

"It looked like a regular twenty when I stuck it in my pocket. After Walter knocked me down, I forgot about it. I ran it through the wash this morning and bingo — hot pink with the picture of Lincoln on the side."

"That's the watermark," Ben said, "part of the security on bills released after '99." Ben held the paper to the light. "I've heard about this. Counterfeiters bleach a lower denomination bill — this was a five spot, then they print over it. It doesn't work all the time. People are pretty savvy at detecting counterfeits these days, but with the festival chaos, this would be the perfect place to pass these around."

"So, this whole thing, the robberies, the murder, it's all maybe tied to counterfeiting?" I said.

"It looks that way," Ben said.

Patrice lifted Ernie into her lap and frowned at the bill. "And what's with the crappy ink? In training, they told us most of them use really good ink."

"I wouldn't have pegged Walter von Dickel for a counterfeiter," Ben said.

"And why rob the bank and all the other places?" Kitty looked puzzled.

"Walter didn't ask for cash at the bank. He asked for twenties. Very specific." I pointed to the bill. "Maybe he robbed the bank to get this back. Maybe there's more of them, and that's what he's after with all the robberies." I peered at tiny scribbles in the bill's margin. "What's that?"

We all leaned closer. I sucked in a breath.

"Dude," Patrice said, "it says 'help.' "

At that moment we heard Verna's creaky voice from the auditorium. "Ben! Hurry!"

We all ran to the stage. We found Verna alone and crouched behind the florist counter. She pointed at the center aisle.

The pony-tailed man wobbled there on shaky legs. A broad red stain bloomed over his white shirt. He took several staggering steps toward us. His gun drooped at his side.

"Coooauuuuch," he moaned and gave a last gurgling breath.

He collapsed.

"Did he say couch?" Kitty said. "Does he want us to take him to the couch?"

I said, "I think he said Coach."

"Elk County Sheriff!" Ben aimed his service pistol at the man and ran toward him. "Sit up and kick the gun toward me with your foot."

The man lay motionless; his blank face aimed toward my enchanted chandelier.

"After everyone left —" Verna's voice shook, and she patted her chest. "He burst in through there." She pointed at the lobby doors.

In the aisle, Ben knocked the man's gun away with his foot. He felt his neck then listened at his chest. With his thumb, he slid the man's lower lip down and peeked at his teeth and gums.

"He's dead." Ben stood.

I stared at the stain spreading beneath the body.

"Oh, my stars," Verna said.

"No way." Patrice scooped Ernie up and clutched him to her chest.

"Good Godfreys, right here in the Egyptian," Kitty whispered.

Gun still drawn, Ben jogged toward the lobby. "Kate, watch the body. You're in charge."

I hiccupped and stared at the dead man.

After a few long minutes during which none of us talked or moved, Ben strode back down the aisle to the stage. "The area's clear. Blood trail tells me he was shot in the alley."

Chills rolled up my spine and goose-bumps exploded on both my arms. My alley.

"I told you a guy was here today — by my stairs," I said, "right before rehearsal. He had a shaved head and a snake tattoo." I poked a finger at the back of my head. "And the Bill Clinton mask. He wore a Devil's Cheerleaders jacket."

"I saw that same man out front talking with him." Verna pointed to the dead man. "Arguing, I think, when I came in."

Kitty said to me, "I didn't tell you, but someone in one of those Cheerleader from Hell jackets followed me out at the mall last night at dinnertime. I asked him if he wanted an autograph, but he just walked away. He had that tattoo on his head, too."

My body tensed. "Kitty, you need to be careful. This situation is dangerous."

Ben raised an eyebrow, and his eyes locked on mine. "That's Snake," Ben said. "He runs the Cheerleaders. And I'll say it's dangerous."

While Ben guarded the body, Patrice took

Ernie back to the light booth, and Verna, Kitty, and I moved to the lobby to wait for the homicide squad.

Seventeen

State troopers appeared at the lobby door within five minutes, followed by Elvis-Presley. I felt my jaw drop.

The King stepped inside. He looked from Kitty to me, and his eyes narrowed. "What'd you do to this one?"

"I'll be jiggered," Kitty muttered. "I really must call Roland and see what the stars are doing."

"Just when you think you've seen it all," Verna said.

"What?" Elvis said. "You all got a problem with this?"

It took a minute to find my voice. "No, you just, you — you look like . . . *Elvis.*"

"Thank you." The King adjusted his shower cap over his black acrylic pompadour. He zipped his white sequined jumpsuit to the neck, encasing a flabby, hairless chest. "I'm doing my act at the Sausage Festival today. My wig's fastened on with spirit gum. I didn't have time to take it off."

The King plopped his tackle box on a gurney and clipped a black service belt over his white studded vinyl one. Elvis-Presley Zowicki and a trooper wheeled their cart past the concession stand. I locked the door behind them.

"Elvis, dear, you don't happen to be a puppeteer, do you?" Verna said.

Elvis ignored everyone without a badge and headed for the body. We trailed him down the aisle.

He bent over the wound, then straightened and tugged his rubber gloves into place.

"It looks like the same small caliber bullet as Fred Schnebbly's. I won't be sure until we get the ballistics back, but I'm betting it's the same gun."

Ben held a wallet in his hands. He clicked his radio. "Eunice ran the driver's license. It's a fake. A damn good one."

We all looked at the pony-tailed man.

"Land sakes," Verna said.

"Run his prints before you do ballistics. I need to know who he is ASAP," Ben said.

Patrice walked toward us, hugging Ernie to her chest. She ogled Elvis's bellbottoms. "Dude! Amazing suit."

Charlene appeared at the back of the theatre. Her lemon-yellow sweatsuit looked cheerful and out of place in the grim scene. "I saw the police cars and a meat wagon. I had to use my key — what the hell happened?"

She stared at the body of the pony-tailed man in the center aisle. "Oh boy."

"Oh boy, is right," I said. I waited for a hiccup that never came.

Elvis's polyester jumpsuit strained to contain his wide hips when he knelt beside the body. "Get these people out of this room, now!" He stabbed a gloved finger at Ernie. "And that . . . dog!"

Ernie shot off a growly bark and squirmed. I lifted him from Patrice's arms.

Ben crossed to me. "I don't want you staying upstairs until I find this biker. Whatever he wants, he means business."

"You can stay at the Senior Center with me," Kitty said. "It's got great security. I could spruce up your wardrobe — give you some makeup tips and extra clothes and whatnot."

My eyelid twitched, and I suppressed a hiccup.

"Or you can stay with me," Charlene said. "My place has great security."

"The Senior Center doesn't allow pets." Verna leaned toward Kitty. "And you and I might have some . . . plans."

139

Kitty paused. "Well, okay then."

Kitty grabbed the remaining Godivas, and she and Verna headed backstage. Patrice stuffed her laptop in her backpack and left for home. Charlene and I climbed the inside stairs with Ernie in tow.

I stood at my armoire and tried to decide what to take to Charlene's.

In a few minutes Ben appeared at my door. He held a plastic evidence bag containing the counterfeit bill.

"I'd feel better if you stayed with me." His blue-gray eyes darkened to a deep ocean tone. "A lot better. You would, too. I promise."

My heart leapt into my throat, and a tingle worked its way out from the core of my body to all my extremities, even my hair follicles tingled. And my big toes. Boy howdy.

When I could talk again, I said, "I thought we weren't going to, you know," I fumbled around for the right words, ". . . get serious . . . until after the primary."

We'd danced around the subject of a real relationship again for the last six months, but when I took the auxiliary deputy job in the middle of an election campaign, we'd put a hold on any potential two-stepping.

Ben crossed the room, leaned close, and put his arms around me. He inhaled the scent of my hair.

"This stupid election can't come fast enough," he said.

"I know." I shut my eyes and listened to the comforting thud that was Ben for a few heartbeats. We snuck a long, deep kiss. "We can wait. As long as Schwenck's gunning for you in the primary, you don't want to give him any more ammo."

"I don't know." Ben gazed into my eyes. "Maybe I should fire you."

"Ha, ha," I said. The last man who fired me ended up dead in my trunk, but I opted not to remind him. Instead I rolled my eyes and sighed. "I need the money. Besides, I like working for the department — aside from the outfit."

"Two and a half weeks and the primary's over." Ben locked onto me with those eyes. "If I win that, I'm uncontested, then if you're ready to . . . get serious, I sure am."

My engine revved, and another tingle shot through me. I ran a finger along Ben's jaw line and smiled.

He watched me load my ugly auxiliary deputy uniform into my overnight bag, followed by my even uglier law enforcement shoes.

"Maybe you should skip crowd control

tomorrow," he said. "It could be dangerous."

I raised my eyebrows. "Do I feel a snort
coming on?"

He held his palms up. "It's not that you
couldn't handle it. I'd just feel better if you
were fully trained. And armed."

I smiled.

"Well, maybe not armed . . ."

I stuffed a couple of T-shirts and a pair of
pajama bottoms into my bag. "Crowd control has one redeeming factor — the crowd."

"Good point," Ben said. "I know you can
handle yourself, but I just want you to be
safe."

"I need to change my clothes," I said.

Ben leaned against the door frame. He
folded his arms and grinned his lopsided
smile. "Fantastic."

I flapped a hand at him. "Go talk to Charlene a minute."

I slid into clean jeans and a tank top. I
pulled on a white button-down shirt and
left it open. I reached for my Stuart Weitzman's.

I stuck one foot inside and wiggled my
toes.

"Ben!" I shrieked.

He charged into the room with Charlene
tight at his heels. Ernie scooted around

142

them and watched me.

With two fingers I waved a yellow square of paper. "Look at this! I found this in my boot. My boot that was at Walter's!"

We peered at the twenty or so strings of numbers and letters, handwritten, very small.

"Looks like code numbers," Ben said.

"I think I know what these are." I waved the Post-It in the air. "Where's that bill?"

Ben held up the evidence bag containing the counterfeit twenty.

I pointed. "Serial numbers. See? And this one's on the list. This had to be what Bill Clinton wanted last night — what they ransacked Walter's apartment for."

"And I let your boot leave the crime scene." Ben rubbed his temples. "Albert Schwenck finds out, he'll have to change his boxer shorts."

"Hey, the tech guys released it," Charlene said. "Not your fault."

"I'm the sheriff. Everything's my fault." Ben looked out the window. Two officers stretched a measuring tape at the far end of the alley. "Counterfeiting, God. With that many serial numbers, something big is up. I'd better call the Secret Service."

Charlene caught my eye. I looked away

and shifted my weight from one sock to the other.

"Great," I said. "The Secret Service."

Kitty and Verna crowded into the room. We showed them the numbers from my boot.

"You'd better be careful." Verna pointed at the scrap of paper. "Whoever broke in will still be wanting that list."

"Wow, this is exciting!" Kitty said. "It's like my movie, *Mayhem in Manhattan,* what with the robberies, and the unidentified dead man, and so forth."

"Yes, but our dead guy is a hit man," I said, "*Mayhem in Manhattan'*s dead guy is an undercover government agent."

We all looked at each other.

Ben swallowed hard and stared at the paper with all the tiny serial numbers, then at me.

"Oh shit," Ben said.

EIGHTEEN

I loaded Ernie's Scooby Doo lunch box with a day's worth of kibbles, Milk-Bones, and his favorite squeaky toy, and we headed downstairs. Ben left with my confiscated boots, the phony twenty, the Post-It, and the heartfelt hope that the pony-tailed man would turn out to be a hit man, a career counterfeiter, a runaway Ukrainian trapeze artist, anything but a federal agent.

I couldn't have agreed more.

Charlene and I stood on the sidewalk beneath the humiliating marquee, "THANK YOU MUDD LAKE FOR A GREAT BENEFIT!"

"What do you know about the Devil's Cheerleaders?" I said.

"I've defended just about every one of them," Charlene said. "They're into everything from dealing drugs to boosting cars. The guy you're talking about with the snake tattoo is Jamie Kahn. Snake's your basic car

145

thief. Doesn't have the smarts God gave a bag of jelly doughnuts."

"Is he clever enough to do counterfeit bills?" I said.

"Screwed up counterfeit bills with 'help' written on them? Maybe." She waited a beat. "I doubt it."

"I remember I heard a motorcycle at Walter's apartment," I said. "And the one guy I saw wore a denim jacket. He could've been a Cheerleader. I never saw his back."

"Ben's working on warrants for the Cheerleaders' clubhouse out at the campgrounds," Charlene said. "What he has is pretty sketchy. When the Secret Service shows up, they'll get it done."

"Great." I shifted my weight and fidgeted.

"Wasn't that guy you dated back in Chicago a Secret Service Agent?" Charlene's intelligent brown eyes bore into me. "Didn't he investigate counterfeiting?"

"I didn't really *date* him. It was more," I thought of the white-hot relationship I'd had with Jack Donner and felt my face grow warm, "a physical thing."

Charlene scooted closer. "Ooh! Give me the skanky, tabloid version of you and this hottie."

I sighed. "I met Jack Donner three years

ago," I said, "right after I split up with Andy."

"The King is definitely not puppeteer material," Kitty said. She and Verna joined us under the marquee. Kitty brightened. "Ooh, are we talking about Andy?"

Verna turned to me. "Andy? Wasn't he that nice homosexual boy you were married to?"

"Oh, darling sweet Andy," Kitty said. Her eyes got a far away misty look as she remembered my ex-husband. "I really miss him. His fashion sense was stellar. His floral arrangements, simply exquisite."

"Leave it to Andy." Charlene shook her head. "Two sessions with a hypnotist, and he comes back gayer than a Rose Bowl parade float."

"He just wanted to quit smoking," I said. "Something went haywire."

"You either are gay, or you aren't. In a heterosexual male, something doesn't just go haywire." Charlene tickled the space between us and made little quote signs around "haywire."

I lifted my palms in the mild spring air. "Don't expect me to explain it."

Nothing like one's spouse leaping out the backdoor of his sexual closet to make a girl saddle up and ride the first bad boy she sees. And what a bad, bad boy. Jack Donner. I tugged my brain and body back to the present.

We followed Verna and Kitty to Verna's beetle.

"I'll watch out for the crooks and whatnot on the way home," Kitty said. She climbed into the passenger seat. "I'm still bounty-hunting, so I need to stay sharp. I'll let you know if I catch Walter."

I lifted Kitty's droopy cardigan back onto her shoulder. Beneath her makeup, she looked tired and more than a little stressed.

"It's been a long couple of days," I said. "You ladies go back to the Senior Center and get some rest. Charlene and I have an errand to run." I closed the door for Kitty.

"Shoe shopping?" Charlene looked at me.

"Cheerleader shopping."

We opted for one car and drove my Riviera out to Charlene's condo. We stashed my overnight bag in the guestroom and left Ernie squeaking his rubber cheeseburger in the middle of the queen-sized guest bed.

"You don't have to come with me," I said.

I squirted more hot sauce on my last bite of carry-out taco. The contents of Charlene's junk drawer lay spread out in front of us on her granite breakfast bar.

"I could have sworn I had a pepper spray

in here." She pawed through match packs, candy mints, and paper-swathed chopsticks from Wong's Chop Suey.

"Seriously." I wadded up my taco wrapper and tossed it in her trash can. "I can do this by myself. I just want this resolved."

Charlene slid her junk drawer back in its slot. "Resolved before the Secret Service gets here?"

"No. Maybe. I don't know . . . I just — I have a feeling about that bill. I think Walter meant it as a message for me."

Charlene slid her drawer back into its slot. "And stealing your money and slamming you into a funnel cake trailer aren't messages?"

I stuck my head in my purse. I found my own canister of pepper spray buried under my compact and hairbrush.

"Oh, look. I'm armed!" I clipped it to my belt, raised my elbows, and twirled around.

"Did you ever use that thing?" Charlene eyed the tiny red canister hanging from my belt.

"The point is not to have to use it."

My cell phone chirped out the *Little Shop* theme.

"I'm out at Zero's." Patrice yelled over raucous background noise. "I was right. Tuesday's still Bike Night. The place is crawling with Devil's Cheerleaders, at least a dozen of them."

"Hang on, Patrice." I covered the phone. "How many Cheerleaders do you think there are, Charlene?"

"A dozen maybe?"

"The guy with the cobra on his head is here. He's all gigged up about some new business plan. He's using words like 'corporate infrastructure,' " Patrice said. "How weird is that?"

"Call me right away if they leave," I said. "Especially him."

"Will do." Patrice hung up.

I grabbed my black windbreaker and scratched Ernie behind the ears. He growled, wagged his tail, and gulped his squeaky toy deeper in his jaws.

I sighed, gave him another pat, and headed down the hall.

I pulled open Charlene's front door. "I can do this alone, really."

Charlene tossed a kitchen knife in her big Louis Vuitton purse. "Like hell you can."

We headed for the Devil's clubhouse.

NINETEEN

Fifteen minutes later we bumped down a potholed dirt driveway. A faded wooden sign, "Starlight Dunes Campground," dangled from a bit of rusted chain. Sloppy red letters, "DEVILS CHEARLEEDERS KEEP OUT" obliterated the sky blue words.

Charlene stared at the misspelled name scrawled over the rotting wood. "I told you, these guys — not so swift."

"We'll just look around, see if we find anything concrete that lets Ben get a warrant. Then we'll get out," I said.

I eased the car down the muddy path until it faded into two ruts in the weedy overgrowth. We rounded a bend in the narrow road, and my phone rang. We both jumped.

"Hey, Kate? Kitty's —" Patrice's voice cut out, and my cell gave a beep.

I looked at it: *No service.*

Charlene pulled out her phone. "Mine's

out of service range, too."

I eased the car deep behind the scrubby bushes and blocked it from sight. I left the keys in the ignition in case we needed a fast getaway, and we climbed out. Charlene followed close behind as I walked to the grimy window. I took a deep breath, cupped my hands around my eyes, and peered inside.

"I don't see any funny money or geezers or anything, do you?" Charlene pressed her forehead to the glass beside me.

"Not yet," I said.

The clubhouse held a shabby pool table. A keg sweated in a watery barrel of ice. A ragged Jolly Roger sagged behind an old door propped on cinder blocks — a makeshift bar. Battered folding tables and metal chairs were scattered around the room.

"No murder weapons or missing people anyplace in sight," Charlene said. "Let's go." She stepped away from the window.

"Wait." I squinted at the dim interior. "Is that a door back there? I'm going around."

At the side of the building, I picked through overgrown brush and sidestepped chunks of broken brick that had fallen from the building's foundation.

Charlene trailed behind, punching her cell phone. "Still no signal," she muttered.

At the back, next to a large pile of trash,

we found a second window. I rubbed dust and grime off the glass with my sleeve, then leaned closer. I gasped.

"What?" Charlene leaned in beside me.

I pointed. "Geezer alert!"

Walter von Dickel craned his neck and peered at us over a stack of U-Haul boxes.

He still wore the XXXL Phish T-shirt, too big for him jeans, and his floppy slippers. Gray duct tape lashed his arms and legs to a weathered Adirondack chair.

I held a finger up, ran around the building, and tried the door. I trotted back and tugged at the front window on the way. Both were locked.

Charlene yanked at the crumbling sash of the storeroom window. It didn't budge.

I grabbed a rock the size of a grapefruit and hurled it through the glass.

"Oh Jeeze," Charlene said.

"I'll go in — you keep watch." I reached through the jagged hole and twisted the latch. "Give me your knife."

I lifted the sash and wriggled inside.

"Hurry up." Walter squinted at me. "I gotta pee like a racehorse," he squawked.

I knelt beside his chair and sawed across the bindings on one arm. I worked on the other while Walter ripped the tape off his bony legs.

I listened to the rumble of the approaching train. Outside the broken storeroom window I could see Charlene on the small slope behind the building. She stared toward the road. The train chugged closer.

I froze. A chill raced up my spine and passed my sinking stomach on its way down the body escalator. My heart provided a loud tom-tom beat to my shifting insides.

We were in the woods, miles from any train tracks. An ear-splitting racket filled the air, and the ground shook beneath our feet.

"Kate, come on. Get out of there!" Charlene yelled, her voice almost drowned out by the howling grumble of engines. She scrambled over the hill.

"Those cheap bastards used tattoo ink," Walter said. "The Coach is gonna kill us all."

"We'll get you back to town, and you can give a statem—"

Walter reached in the nearest U-Haul box, pulled out an ouzo bottle, and clocked me in the side of the head.

I staggered sideways, lost my balance, and hit the dusty wood floor. I got to my feet in time to see Walter combat roll out the open window.

I ran to it. I rubbed my aching temple and stuck my head out. Charlene had dis-

154

appeared over the crest of the slope, and Walter was nowhere in sight.

The roar became unbearable. I scooted to the front window and peeked out. A million single points of light lit up the rutted driveway, but not in the good way.

"Holy jeeze," I whispered. I stared as motorcycles one-by-one revved and rolled under the roof of the big wooden picnic shelter.

Behind all the leather and rubber and chrome and satanic delinquency that was the Devil's Cheerleaders came a car — a big white convertible car, circa 1974.

"Oh, dear God," I said.

Verna backed onto a patch of gravel in front of the shelter, and Kitty opened the passenger door.

She'd added skin-tight leather pants, motorcycle boots, and a jacket with chains to her Dog the Bounty Hunter ensemble. The pants squeezed at her spreading middle, and the chains appeared to be the kind that swagged the light fixture over Kitty's dinette set.

I pulled away from the window, leaned my head against the weathered paneling, and hiccupped.

I needed a plan. I thought of the ouzo. I glanced around at the tables littered with playing cards and overflowing ashtrays. I snatched a lighter.

"We're looking for a Mr. Harpo." Verna clutched her big needlepoint purse under her arm and made her way around the car. "His mother said we'd find him out here."

Kitty said, "I want someone to give me motorcycle lessons. It's for a picture I'll be filming." She straightened her narrow shoulders. "For my Hollywood comeback."

I backed against the window frame. "Oh Jeeze, Oh Jeeze . . ."

I felt cold sweat seeping through the pores of my forehead.

I spotted the Jolly Roger hanging on the clubhouse wall. I ran to it and ripped it into several shreds of fabric. I scooted across the clubhouse and slipped into the storeroom. I poured ouzo on the bare floor and watched it soak into the brittle planks. I grabbed another bottle, dumped it. Then another. The smell of licorice and alcohol filled the air. I stuffed tattered strips of Jolly Roger fabric into another ouzo bottle and turned the bottle until they were soaked.

"Is Mr. Harpo, here?" Verna said. Her crinkly voice, even more fragile than usual.

Clutching my Molotov ouzo bottle, I ran to the window. Charlene's face popped up inches from mine.

I staggered backward.

"Jeeze, you scared the livin' crap out of me!" I hissed.

"My livin' crap packed up and left five minutes ago. What are we going to do?" Charlene said.

"Stand back." I motioned her away from the window.

I lit a shred of Jolly Roger and tossed it on the liquor soaked floor. A whooshing flame enveloped the wood, and it ignited like a tray full of flaming Greek sausage. I clutched the ouzo bottle in one hand and the lighter in the other and scrambled out the window.

I peeked around the building. The bikers had formed a tight circle around Kitty and Verna.

A Cheerleader sniffed the air. "What's that smell?"

Heads poked up and noses twitched, but the men stayed where they were.

I glanced around for the best target for my bottle — the garbage pile. I lit the rag and, after long seconds, it flamed up.

"Throw it!" Charlene said.

"Get ready to run!" I flung the bottle and smashed it into the wall above the trash. Liquid flame rolled down the peeling paint.

A loud explosion rocked through the

debris and cans and papers flew into the air. Burning bits of paper mingled with spray cans and garbage and rained down from the dusky sky. Charlene grabbed my arm, and we scooted around the far side of the clubhouse, dodging the falling debris as we ran.

The bikers scrambled toward the smoke and noise.

Kitty leapt behind the wheel of the Land Yacht and Verna, moving much faster than I would have dreamt possible, dove into the passenger side.

"Wait!" I scooted into the seat behind Verna, and Charlene threw herself in behind Kitty.

"Oh my stars," Verna said, "where did you come from?"

"Hit it," I yelled.

Kitty shoved the transmission into gear and stomped on the gas.

The car flew backward, and the big rear bumper slammed into a rickety support post. We jerked back in our seats. A loud cracking sound seemed to come from all around us.

"Darn it all," Kitty hollered. "I meant to hit drive!" She stepped on the pedal, and we continued in reverse. Beside us, the post cracked apart and fell away from the roof.

It smacked the ground, narrowly missing our rear bumper.

We all twisted around and looked up. The big wooden roof teetered precariously.

Verna reached over, slammed the car into drive and shoved her orthopedic shoe on top of Kitty's boot.

The car lurched forward and growled. It heaved, then stopped moving, and we heard the sound of tires spinning in mud. Dirt and gravel shot out behind us as the shelter gave off a massive cracking sound. The other front post snapped in half and fell inward. It narrowly missed the hood.

"Holy crap!" I yelled.

Bikers swarmed toward us from behind the clubhouse.

"Kill those stupid bitches," someone yelled.

"We can't murder until we get our certificates," a voice said.

"Screw that. Let's kill 'em!" hollered another.

They charged us.

Several loud snapping and popping sounds, then a whoosh of air rocked the car as the roof crunched down on the Devil's motorcycles like a stomp of the foot from God. The eave caught the rear bumper of the car, and we rocked deeper into the gravel and mud. We jerked again as the remains of the building slid off the trunk.

An unending sea of meaty, irate bikers seethed toward us.

Kitty floored it, and the wheels spun watery gravel and clumps of mud.

"Lord in heaven," Verna squealed.

Charlene punched at her cell buttons and shook it in the air. "I defended you guys. Give us a break," she yelled through our closed window.

I hiccupped and dug frantically at my hip. I unhooked my pathetically small and probably expired canister of pepper spray.

I was sure we were dead.

Just then, the clubhouse exploded behind us into a ball of blue flame.

"Go on. I'll get them!" a big, grizzly biker hollered.

All but the one ran back toward the clubhouse.

Kitty rocked the car forward, then back. This sent us deeper. The lone, grizzly biker appeared in the rearview mirror. I rolled down the window and pressed the button on my pepper spray. It tinkled into the air. The stream landed in the mud far short of its target.

Verna squinted through her bifocals at the rear view mirror. She grabbed my arm.

"Kate! Don't!"

The biker kicked a board out of his way and shoved hard at our trunk.

"Hit it!" he croaked in a raspy whisper.

Kitty pressed the accelerator, and we rocketed free of the mud. The big tires caught, and we barreled down the dirt service road.

"Hot Cha-cha!" Kitty said, "Charlie's Angels . . . Plus one! We're the monkey's eyebrows, aren't we?"

TWENTY

We all gasped for air a bit, then rode in tense silence until we reached the shopping center at the edge of town.

I rubbed my head, then smacked the seat in frustration. "That Walter! I'm going to kill him myself." I thought about the smashed bikes. "If I live that long."

"You saw Walter?" Verna asked.

"Oh, fudge." Kitty turned in her seat. "I missed him."

"Um, the road?" I pointed forward and filled them in on the story. I wrapped up with Walter's ditty about the tattoo ink and "the Coach is gonna kill us all."

Verna said, "The Coach? Who would that be?"

"It might be a nickname. The Oldsmobile played sports. Did anyone call him the Coach, darling?" Kitty swiveled her head around and the big car swerved. "Or maybe the Cadillac? He played polo sometimes."

Kitty's seven husbands stayed parked in her big lot of memories only by their cars.

"The Olds was Harry, and the Caddy's name was Stu." I winced as Verna dove for the steering wheel. "No one called either of them the Coach." I groaned. "Oh no! *My* car's back there at the campground!"

"Did you cut back on auto insurance, like you did the theatre coverage?" Kitty wanted to know.

I frowned and nodded.

Verna gripped the wheel and steered us to our side of the yellow line. "We'd better pull off at Petey's Pita, dear," she said. "I could use some tea."

We'd just gotten our drinks and seated ourselves at the garishly lit Petey's Pita when Charlene spotted something over my shoulder.

"Uh oh," she said. "Trouble."

I turned in my seat. A Devil's Cheerleader filled the entire doorway. He headed for our table.

"What about the ladies' room? We could hide in there. Call Ben . . ." I got up.

Verna patted my hand. "No, dear. It's okay. This is my Godson, Harpo Pentwood. He's the one who pushed us out of the mud."

The hulking man headed for our table. At

least half the Cheerleaders had that hefty bikers' build, unkempt beard, and scary denim motorcycle jacket, but when he smiled at Verna, Harpo looked more like a badly groomed teddy bear than a delinquent. A white trainee ribbon, the kind a new waitress wears, dangled from his jacket pocket.

Verna got up and held her arms out. "Hello, Harpo sweetheart. And how is your mother?"

The burly man engulfed her in a hug. "Auntie Verna, you scared the dickens out of me. What the heck were you thinking?"

"We didn't intend to cause such trouble," Kitty said. "Although it's quite invigorating, this bounty-hunting and so forth."

"We pulled into Zero's just as you were leaving," Verna said. "We just decided to follow you. It was foolish, I know. So foolish . . ."

"It was kind of a business meeting," Harpo said. "We all left the bar after Snake split."

Verna beamed at him. "Harpo's following in my footsteps."

"Nonsense." Kitty shrugged out of her jacket, and her chains clanked onto the booth. "You were never a motorcyclist."

"Not that," Harpo said. "I'm undercover."

I tried to picture Verna back in the sixties, when she was a missionary in China and did what she called her "undercover government work."

"Uh-oh," Kitty said. "Undercover? Sorry about your motorcycle." Kitty nudged me. "Kate, apologize about his clubhouse."

Something didn't feel right. I furrowed my brow. "Are you with the government?"

The big man looked confused.

"Heavens no, dear," Verna said. "He's with the church. Show them, Harpo."

Harpo stood and unbuttoned his flannel shirt. Underneath he wore a black T-shirt with white print: *I'm a biker, for the love of God!*

"He's infiltrating them for our motorcycle ministry," Verna said.

"I'm making up for my misspent youth." His blue eyes twinkled at the memory of his misspending.

Charlene repeated the last words of his shirt out loud. "For the love of God . . ."

"Exactly," Harpo said.

"So," Charlene said, "what's with the old guy taped up in the storeroom?"

"What old guy? I haven't been allowed in the storeroom yet," Harpo said. He pointed to his ribbon. "I'm still in trainee status. The Cheerleaders have a very strict operational structure."

"Since when?" Charlene wanted to know.

"It's pretty recent. They want to take it to the next level." He tossed my keys on the table. "I don't think they saw the black car. I followed you with it. You'd better hide that whale you're driving, but quick. You're going to have a lot of pissed — sorry Aunt Verna, ticked-off bikers after you."

"Good idea, son." Verna nodded.

"I'll stick with you until you ditch the big car," Harpo said. "Just in case."

Verna followed with Harpo in my car, while I drove the Land Yacht to the loading area in back of Wal-Mart. I eased the big convertible into a space, and Kitty, Charlene, and I got out.

We stood between the vehicles.

"Can we give you a ride somewhere, dear?" Verna reached up and straightened the collar on Harpo's denim jacket.

"No thanks, Aunt Verna," Harpo said. "Mom's picking me up in my car."

Seconds later a blue Taurus driven by a pudgy, gray-haired woman glided up beside us.

A sinking feeling took over in my stomach, and my mouth went dry. While Verna chatted with mother and son, I stole a look at the car's plate. It began with a 'P' or 'F' and was caked with mud — the same as we'd seen on the blue Taurus we'd chased down the highway. This was the getaway car from the bank.

After we dropped Kitty and Verna at the Senior Center and made them promise not to leave or buzz anyone in, Charlene and I headed to her condo.

On the way, I dialed Patrice and told her we were okay.

"I got the skinny on Rhonda," she said. "Nothing on the Internet on her, but at Zero's I found out she hangs out with Snake."

I thanked her and hung up.

When we arrived at the condo, I walked Ernie while Charlene opened the balcony's sliding doors to the unobstructed fifth-floor view of Lake Michigan. We built a crackling fire to fend off the chilly spring air.

Ernie lay sprawled on his back, asleep in front of the hearth. His paws twitched at the ceiling, and he chuffed out low woofing noises.

"Maybe I'm wrong about the blue Taurus. Maybe it's not the getaway car." I stood before Charlene in my baggy uniform trousers.

"And maybe Harpo has Verna horn-swoggled." Charlene knelt and tugged at my pant leg. "You know it's the car." She pinched some fabric. "You have to tell Ben."

"Verna's going to hate me." I turned and Charlene slid a straight pin along the outer seam. "Maybe there's a logical explanation."

"Kate, you have to tell him." She looked up and met my eyes. "You know you do."

I sighed. "First thing tomorrow."

"Okay, then." She nodded. "Next subject: are we replacing Mary? I'll need to fit a costume before the show."

"God, the show." I rubbed my hands over my face. "Opening night and the Crackle-Pops Foundation. It's three days away."

"Hell, what's one less girl singer?" Charlene said. "It's the Players, no one expects them to follow the script. Or you could just cancel the show. Just call the foundation tomorrow." She ran another straight pin into the seam at my hip. "Be done with it."

I groaned. "We can't refund tickets. We lost that money in the robbery, too."

"Oh boy." Charlene tugged the fabric tight across my backside. "I've got a bad feeling about this show."

"I've got a bad feeling about so many things, the show is way down my list," I said.

Less than an hour later, I stood before Charlene again.

"I don't know if Ben will go for these." I

eyed my reflection in the mirrored fireplace surround. "They're kind of form-fitting. And aren't they a little fashion-forward for the Mudd Lake Sheriff's department?"

"The Sheriff's Department consists of two people other than you. And nobody ever sees Eunice. Besides, you're auxiliary. You should have leeway."

I turned around for her. "This much leeway?"

"Oh, yeah. If Ben has a beating heart, he'll want to give you more than leeway," Charlene said.

"I told you, we're on hold," I said.

"Well, these will sure keep him on the line while he's holding," she said. "He's gonna love these on you."

"Is that before or after he arrests me for arson?" I headed for the bedroom.

After slipping into my pj's, I joined Charlene and Ernie in front of the fire.

While I'd been gone, Charlene had poured each of us hefty balloon goblets of Pinot Noir. She eyed me over the rim of her glass. "So tell me about Jack Donner."

"Nothing to tell," I mumbled. I buried my nose in my own glass.

"I just helped you blow up a den of criminals. It was fun, really, but now I'm in danger of losing my life, not to mention my law license. And I'm kind of tired." Charlene stretched her legs in front of the fire and warmed her toes. "So, don't make me cross examine you."

I looked out at the starlit night and watched a distant freighter gliding slow and relentless across the inky waters. "I haven't seen or talked to Jack Donner since I moved back from Chicago. I don't even know where he is."

"So, what made you break it off with him?" Charlene got to her knees and poked at the fire. An explosion of sparks shot up the chimney.

I shifted and held my hands out. The air was about sixty degrees over the water, and the roaring fire felt good, like a fall bonfire.

"Did you ever go out with somebody you knew wasn't good for you? You weren't good for each other, but there was this sort of . . . sort of . . ." I lifted my hands and made a taffy-pulling motion, "draw?"

Charlene shifted her weight and straightened the elastic around the ankle of her chartreuse sweatpants. "Did you forget who you were talking to here? I am the queen of bad relationships."

I patted her knee. "Anyway, I knew it was better to just let it go. I think he did, too."

I looked at the freighter and thought about

how I hadn't returned Jack's calls after I'd moved back to Mudd Lake. Then the calls had stopped.

"You may not know where he is," Charlene said, "but if he's a Fed and that relationship was half of what your face tells me it was —" She refilled her glass. "You can bet he knows where you are."

TWENTY-ONE

The next morning Ben and I stood in front of the smoldering remains of the Cheerleaders' clubhouse.

Ben scanned the charred ruins of the front wall. "So the pony-tailed man was a federal agent — a deep-cover Secret Service operative. He was investigating a tip about a counterfeit ring with ties in Mudd Lake," he said.

I surveyed the debris around us. "And ties to the Cheerleaders, I bet."

"I'm guessing you're right." Ben pointed to the clubhouse. "The fire must've spread from here to the picnic shelter after the explosion."

"Wow," I said. "Freak lightning is a terrible thing."

"Ha, ha." Ben lifted his sunglasses to the top of his head and pinned me with his changeable blue-gray eyes. "Don't press your luck."

I avoided his glare. On the drive out, I'd told him the truth about the bikes and the fire and Walter's escape.

"I'm not real happy, but the property owners are ecstatic," Ben had told me. "They've been too afraid of the Devil's Cheerleaders to file a formal complaint about their squatting."

I eyed the twisted mass of mangled and melted motorcycles under the charred rubble of the shelter.

Ben eyed *me.*

"It's very hard to be mad at you in that outfit. What exactly did you do to your uniform?" His eyes slid to the red heart-shaped bull's-eye that decorated my black baby-doll T-shirt, then down my uniform pants and to my feet. At Charlene's insistence, I'd dumped the clunky requisition shoes for my kitten-heeled Jimmy Choo boots.

I lifted my sunglasses and grinned at him. I had to admit, it was one smokin' uniform.

"That agent, when he died, his last word sounded like 'Coach.' And Walter said, 'the Coach is gonna kill us all.' So, who is this Coach?" I said.

Ben shook his head. "Beats me."

"And what's with all this ouzo?" I said. "The Cheerleaders aren't even Greek."

"And it's in U-Haul boxes." Ben stuck his head through the charred window frame and surveyed the U-Haul logo on a ragged piece of damp cardboard.

"Maybe they stole it," I said.

Ben lifted a blackened piece of wood, and ash swirled into the clear spring air. "No reports have been filed."

I picked up the partial remains of an exploded aerosol can. "Krylon," I said. "Art fixative. That's unusual."

"That's what blew up. Look at this — boxes of it in the trash." He swept his hand toward the garbage area. "Sometimes counterfeiters spray fixative like this on their bills," Ben moved to the charred remains of the doorframe, "to try and hold the color."

"If that's what they did, it sure didn't work. Walter told us they were cheap, that they used tattoo ink," I said. "Did he mean for counterfeiting? Could that be what turned the bill pink?"

"It's the prevailing theory. The Secret Service is testing the bill right now," Ben said.

"The Secret Service is here?" I swallowed. "Already?"

"They sure are. They lost one of their own, and they're here in force." Ben looked toward the driveway. "Right now, as a matter of fact."

Gravel crunched, and a gray sedan bumped across the potholes.

"The Secret Service . . ." I said. My breath caught in my throat, and I stared.

The car disgorged two blue-suited individuals, a man and a woman. Not Jack.

I exhaled.

The Agents-That-Were-Not-Jack approached the clubhouse. The female snapped pictures of the collapsed shelter, the smoking shell of the building, and the fixative shrapnel on the ground.

The male agent stepped over some shredded cardboard and stood in front of us. "This looks like arson," he said.

I moved closer to Ben.

"I'm thinking sabotage. Extensive damage like this," the agent swung his hand across the decimated campground, "you're talking gang war. I guarantee it."

Ben's dimple appeared, and he slipped his sunglasses back over his eyes. "I know these guys," Ben said. "They're always in trouble. Probably just carelessness."

The agent looked around. "No. I'm telling you, your profile is that of a warring gang, probably big, with a serious history of violence. Maybe an ex-Navy SEAL or two."

Ben nodded, and the muscle in his cheek

worked to suppress his grin. "I'll look into it."

The female agent sidled in front of me. Her navy pantsuit bagged at the thighs and crotch, and she wore her hair yanked back in a severe ponytail. She kept her back to us and held a cell phone to her ear.

"Ron," she said to her partner, "Nancy von Dickel-Schnebbly just used her Visa card in Aruba. She's staying at the Siesta Villas down there, and she just bought several items."

"What kind of items?" Ron said.

"Stuff like she's staying a while. Supplies. Toilet paper, coffee, peanut butter, domestic supplies."

The male agent pulled her arm, and the two agents stepped away from us.

I leaned forward to hear better — something about a plan to have Nancy picked up for questioning.

"You don't mind if we take a look around, do you, Williamson?" the male agent said. "We try to help in these . . . rural situations."

"Have at it." Ben walked to the Tahoe. I followed.

"Rural situations . . ." He slapped the buckle together on his shoulder harness. "Do I look like Andy of Mayberry to you?"

I scanned his wavy black hair, square jaw, and lanky build. I thought he did, just a little, but it seemed like a bad thing to mention.

"Not even close," I said.

We bounced down the driveway.

"I can tell you one thing," I said. "Nancy didn't buy those groceries."

We pulled out to the road. "How do you know?"

"Nancy von Dickel and I were best friends," I said.

Ben smiled his quirky smile. "I remember. I spent my entire paper route money for those pumpkin panties."

I ignored that. "The agent said she bought peanut butter. She's deadly allergic to peanuts."

"So, she didn't buy it for herself," Ben said. "Maybe she's with somebody and bought it for them."

"No way. I mean deadly allergic. She won't go near the stuff," I said. "Can you get the number of Siesta Villas?"

We passed Wal-Mart and headed down the bypass ramp toward town. A few minutes later Ben had the number. I grinned at him, punched the code to block my cell's caller ID, then dialed the Siesta Villas. I asked for Nancy Schnebbly's suite.

After a brief one-sided conversation, I hung up.

"Last I knew, Nancy spoke English," I said.

"A lot of hot credit cards get sold down in Mexico. They're harder to track in tourist areas," Ben said.

"Maybe they killed her and sold her card," I said.

Weird old Nancy, we'd read the entire *Chronicles of Narnia* out loud in our secret place behind the library. A sadness washed over me.

"She might not be dead." Ben grabbed my hand and squeezed. "Walter isn't."

"If Walter hits me one more time," I said, "he will be."

Ben patted my hand, then let it go.

I hesitated. "There's one more thing I need to tell you." I'd held it off. Somehow I'd hoped it would go away. But it wouldn't. Verna would hate me, but I had to do it. My heart sank as I told Ben about Harpo and the blue Taurus.

"I think it's the getaway car from the bank," I said.

TWENTY-TWO

A few minutes later, I was slunk low in my seat. I watched through the window while Ben talked to Harpo's mom. He stopped halfway to the car and answered his radio. After talking a few seconds he clicked off.

"Get this. The twenty tested positive for tattoo ink." Ben climbed in and fastened his belt. "That's what turned the bill pink in the wash. They mixed that ink with the really expensive counterfeiting pigments. It gives new meaning to the word cheap."

"And dumb," I said. "So, the Coach is going to kill everybody for that? And he probably shot Fred and the agent. Or Snake did. People don't usually have two nicknames. Snake is behind this, and so is this Coach."

"I don't know who Coach is," Ben said. "But your buddy Harpo? His mom told me where he works. Care to guess?"

That sinking feeling came back. I shrugged.

"Raw-Raw Tattoos." Ben started the car. "We're meeting the agents there, right now."

Minutes later we pulled in a few doors down from a shabby, shack-like storefront. A black sign painted with the now familiar devil-woman hung overhead. She aimed her pom-poms at the name: Raw-Raw Tattoos.

Mudd Lake's only known hooker stood out front, her yellow Lycra mini-dress taut as the wrapper on a Butterball turkey. She watched Ben get out of the car and waddled her three-hundred-pound bulk out of sight at the far corner of the block.

I followed Ben to the shop's window. Inside, Harpo stood behind the counter. A big leather-bound book lay open in front of him. I looked again. If that traditional Christian Hell existed, the televangelist one, chock-full of flying brimstone and molten lava, I'd just earned a one-way pass.

I groaned and rubbed at the back of my neck. It ached from stress or maybe from repeated take-downs at the hands of a wiry eighty-year-old salsa dancer.

Harpo moved the ribbon to mark his place and closed his Bible.

Maybe I could convince Ben to wait. Maybe he'd let me talk to Harpo. "Ben —"

Ben put a finger to his lips and pointed at the front fender of the blue Taurus visible on the far side of the building. "There's the car."

The gray sedan carrying the two agents we'd left at the clubhouse pulled up behind our vehicle. They climbed out and joined us on the sidewalk.

"How about we go in on our own and take him?" the female, Eva, said. "You guys wait outside."

"How about we all take him together?" Ben stepped in front of her and headed through the door.

Harpo looked up. "What can I do for you? Oh, hi, Kate. Everything all — ?"

Eva poked her gun at Harpo's nose. "Federal agents, do not move. This is a raid."

Harpo's brows shot up, and his eyes grew wide. He threw his arms up toward the cracked ceiling. "What? What's wrong? What are you doing? Raid? It's my first day!"

Ben read Harpo his rights while the male agent, Ron, waved a warrant under Harpo's chin, then Ron put his ear against the door to the back room. He listened a few seconds, then rammed his foot into the wood. Splinters flew through the air and the door clacked open. It smacked against the inside plaster and rocked the little building.

Aside from tattoo samples hanging on the

walls, miscellaneous paraphernalia on an old metal shelving unit, and some kind of modified recliner, the back room was empty.

Ron pointed to a clean rectangular area on the dusty tile floor. The shape took up the space of maybe two refrigerators. "Look at this."

He pointed to another square shape surrounded by dust. He snapped photos of both. I took a step forward and tried to guess what was so interesting.

The agent frowned at me and pointed to Eva. "I meant her. I wanted her to see it, not you."

I narrowed my eyes at him. These two were getting on my nerves.

"Cuff the guy, would you, Sheriff?" Ron brushed a hand at Ben. "And can you have your . . . deputy . . . step out of the room? Please? Before she contaminates our evidence."

I cut my eyes at the agents. "I wasn't planning to pee on anything important," I said.

"Very funny. And it's all important," Eva said. She pushed me out of the way. "Very important."

They both turned their backs again. I felt heat rise into my face.

"You know, you could've tried the knob before you kicked the door, *Ron,*" I said.

Ron ignored me. "Eva, check this out."

Ben cuffed Harpo who glared across the room in my direction. "I helped you." He jabbed his chin at the ribbon dangling from his jacket. "I — I'm only a *trainee!*"

Eva held her camera to her face and clicked off several pictures. "These are the right sizes," she said. She pointed to the wall. "And there's the 220 outlet."

"Right sizes for what?" I looked at the boxy shapes surrounded by grime and dust.

She waved her hand over the space. "Off-set press, rack for storing the plates, drying area, maybe even a cutter. A full-blown counterfeiting operation. There's no way to prove it, though. Damn!"

"Sheriff, we picked up your warrant for the Taurus." Eva handed Ben the folded paper.

"We have reason to believe your vehicle was used in a robbery," Ben said to Harpo. "And that it may be related to a homicide."

"That's impossible," Harpo said.

"Kate, is this the man you saw driving the getaway car?" Ben pointed to Harpo.

Harpo looked at me. "Kate? What the dickens is going on here?"

"All I saw was a Bill Clinton mask." I shifted and backed toward the door. "I doubt it was him." I avoided Ben's eyes. "It

183

probably wasn't."

Ben stared at me and waited a few exasperated seconds.

I looked at my feet. "It could've been."

"I don't believe this," Harpo said. "Lord, have mercy."

"Let's take a look at your car." Ben held Harpo by the arm and pulled him out the door.

Ben walked around the Taurus while Harpo glared at me again. "Great pay back. Thanks."

Ben looked at the plate. "Was this the car?"

I'd only seen the one letter, the 'P' or 'F' and that matched. The mud smeared across the surface looked intentional, identical to the way I remembered it. I nodded. "Uh-huh."

"Thanks again." Harpo jerked his head at the tattoo parlor. "I've only been here a couple of hours."

"This is about your car, now. Let's check the trunk." Ben snapped on rubber gloves and lifted the lid.

He rummaged around and produced a crumpled IGA bag.

"Bingo." He held it out.

Tightly banded stacks of twenty-dollar bills filled the bag. The bands were printed with "Mudd Lake Savings."

Ben showed the bag to Harpo. His bushy eyebrows furrowed.

"That isn't mine!" he said. "I've never seen that before in my life."

"Uh-huh," Ben said. He set the bag on the car's roof.

"Ben, the benefit money isn't there, is it? Or the Festival money?" I walked around to the trunk. "Maybe somebody put that in his car to make him look bad."

"They did a good job," Ben said. He reached around and pulled something else out of the trunk. A handgun. "Ever seen this before?"

The color drained from Harpo's face. "I've never seen any of this before." Harpo looked at me. "I helped you. Can't you do something?"

"Now, wait a second, I know it wasn't him in the alley," I said. "That guy had a shaved head and a snake tattoo. Not to mention the Bill Clinton mask."

Eva and Ron walked up behind Ben. "That sounds like the shop's owner, Snake. They're probably partners."

Ron reached in the trunk. "And look here," he said. He held up an empty bottle of tattoo ink. "Eva, check a couple of those bills."

Eva took the bag from the roof and tugged a twenty out of a packet. She held a bill up to the light and smiled. "We have ourselves a counterfeiter. And an agent killer."

The trunk held at least a dozen more ink bottles, all of them empty, all of them marked green.

"Harpo Pentwood, you're under arrest for accessory to robbery and suspicion of murder," Ben said.

"And we have a few charges of our own," Eva said.

She turned to Ron. "Once we find his partner, we'll get the press and the plates. Jack's going to love this. He'll find out where that equipment is." She pointed at Harpo. "This guy is going down. You can take that to the bank — the Mudd Lake Savings Bank." She chuckled.

Jack? No need to get nervous. Lots of Jacks in the world. I hiccupped.

I walked to the Tahoe and sat down. I pulled out my cell and punched two digits of Verna's number, then cancelled and slipped my phone back in my purse.

What would I tell her? He'd probably saved our lives, and this is how he gets paid back?

I climbed out of the car. Harpo sat cuffed in the back seat of the sedan. He sent me a look that made my chest ache, part pity, part anger, part shock.

Harpo leaned out. "I'm praying for you," he said. "But you're making it mighty hard."

"I believe you didn't know about this, Harpo." I patted his arm. "I think you're being framed."

"What the hell are you doing?" Eva scowled at me. "Don't touch that prisoner."

I yanked my hand away and stumbled backward.

Ben sighed and ran his hand through his hair.

"Sheriff, get her out of here, would you?" Ron cut in front of me and slammed the back door to the sedan.

Ben straightened his broad shoulders and took a step forward. "If it wasn't for her, you wouldn't have an arrest," Ben said. "Plus she discovered your counterfeit bill, and the serial numbers." He glared at the agents.

Ron folded his arms over his chest. "We would have found them."

"Not in my Stuart Weitzman boot, you wouldn't have." I rammed my hands into my hips and squinted at them.

They both squinted back.

"Anyway, I'll thank you to treat my deputy with respect." Ben shot me a look. "No matter how crazy she makes you."

I stomped back to the Tahoe and tossed myself in the passenger seat again. I pulled out my grocery pad and jotted questions while I tried not to fume. Why did Walter run? Who framed Harpo? Where was Nancy? Who killed Fred? And who the heck was Coach? I bent my head and clutched fistfuls of hair. I was busy pulling it sideways with my eyes shut, yanking my head back and forth, when Ben climbed in the car.

"Arrrgh!"

"Oh, don't take them seriously," Ben said.

"It's not that," I said. "It's this — this has so many moving parts!"

"The feds say Harpo is a kingpin in the Cheerleader's multi-national counterfeiting operation," Ben said.

I thought of Charlene's comment. The top Cheerleader was as dumb as jelly dough-nuts. "Multinational counterfeiting? I bet most of them wouldn't know where to sign their own name on a check." I pointed to the sedan. "And he's only a trainee."

"It feels hinky to me, too," Ben said. "But look at the evidence."

"Okay, forget that trainee spiel and look at facts," I said. "Let's say it's his first day at Raw-Raw. You can verify whether he's been working here, right?"

"Yeah, so?" Ben turned the ignition.

"Did you see that dust on the floor? That counterfeiting equipment had to be there months before it was moved." I slapped the dash. "If it's his first day, that's not even a good frame-up."

Ben frowned. "Damn good frame on the car, though." Ben caught my eye. "*If* it's a frame. He still could have been involved with the counterfeiting, you know, even if he didn't work here."

I banged the dash, this time with my fist. "It's so obvious that it's a frame."

"This thing gets weirder and weirder." Ben pulled onto the highway. "I'm kind of glad Jack Donner's here," he said. "Maybe with his resources, he can put all these pieces together."

My breath caught in my throat again, and my voice squeaked. "Did you say Jack Donner?"

"Yeah." Ben nodded. "He's the head of the Secret Service team. Eva and Ron and the ten or so swarming my office right now, they all report to him. Jack's the only decent one in the whole bunch. Nice teeth, too. Not even caps."

I hiccupped.

Ben looked over at me. "What's got into you?"

189

I stared at my watch. "Oh, gee! Would you look at the time?" I hiccupped again. "I've got to get to the festival. The Fishing Derby starts in an hour. Drop me at Charlene's, would you?"

TWENTY-THREE

Before I got out, I turned to Ben. "I'm going to do what I can for Harpo," I said. "And not just because of Verna. Whoever framed him today may have done it because they knew he helped us last night. I owe it to him to undo this stupid thing."

"Remember, it's his Taurus," Ben said. "His Taurus full of guns and money, I might add. That's hard to undo."

I shook my head. "I haven't figured that part out yet, but I will."

Ben put his head down on the steering wheel. His eyes slid in my direction. "Couldn't you just . . . I don't know . . . knit or something?" he said.

"Not unless I can knit Harpo a hacksaw."

I hiccupped, patted Ben's arm, and trotted up the steps to Charlene's. I took Ernie out for a quick walk, grabbed a leftover taco, and dialed the theatre phone. I punched the remote code for messages and munched my taco while I listened. After a dozen or so requests for tickets and two solicitation calls, the CracklePops Foundation came on verifying their ten front-row seats for Friday night. Then Joe Splotski's voice came on the line.

"Hey, Deadbeat! I didn't get your money. Drive my puppets back to Detroit by noon tomorrow, or I'll send somebody to get them." It was date-stamped yesterday.

I stabbed the end button and looked at my watch: 11:45.

Perfect. Just perfect.

I drove to the Egyptian and parked. Grabbing my cell, I clipped it to my belt and shoved my purse under the car seat. Scanning the street for bad guys and now for Jack Donner, too, I walked to the festival. I counted six Albert Schwenck for Sheriff posters on the way.

A few small crafts already trolled the waterfront. They motored toward the area marked off by the Fishing Derby buoys. At the Oom-Pah-Pah tent I scanned the registration forms to see how many boats we could expect. Ben said to plan for two cars and a trailer for each boat registered.

Juan sat at the money table behind the open strong box. "They make me take the cash today for the Ugly Man Derby."

A bowl of sudsy water and a bottle of Tide sat beside him.

"I have to dip the money in the soap. Sometimes it turns pink. I have to send them over there to the suits." He mumbled that Spanish thing that sounded like Mercury in retrograde.

Juan pointed to a table. Two agents sat behind a mound of reports and a stack of pink tipped bills. About a dozen irate-looking townspeople lined up in front of them.

"Is a waste of time, if you ask me — this soap-dipping business." Juan held a bill up to the light and squinted at it.

I hunched down and followed his gaze.

"You have good peepers, you can see the leetle guy." He pointed. "Right here."

Lincoln's face showed through at the side, Ulysses S. Grant in the center, just like before. "It's a fake," I said.

A man in a feed-cap and overalls standing in front of Juan said, "Dip it, just to be sure. I don't want to have to turn it in if it ain't a fake."

"Is a fake," Juan said. "I'm not dippin' it. I don't need no dishpan hands from the Ugly Man Festival, you know?"

The man in the feed-cap bristled. "Who you callin' ugly?"

Juan sighed. "I gonna dip it, but it's a waste. You gotta go see the suits."

I glanced over. Eva and Ron had joined the other agents at the table.

Juan stuck a corner of the bill in the soapy water and waited.

Nothing happened.

I bent over and squinted at the twenty. "Why doesn't it turn colors?"

Juan shrugged and stared at the bowl. "I'm just a kielbasa cook. You got me."

I took the bowl of detergent and the bill over to the agents. The feed-capped man followed me.

"Hey Ron?" I twisted Ron's copy of the serial numbers and pointed to the sequence from the bill. "This serial number matches one from the list, and it has the wrong watermark, but this bill doesn't turn pink."

Ron stared at the twenty. "Give me that." He motioned to Eva and snatched the bowl containing the soggy bill from my hand.

He turned his back to me, and the two huddled with the other agents. Ron turned still holding the bowl. "Thanks for bringing this to our attention."

The feed-capped man plucked the bill from the water. "It don't turn colors, it ain't a fake. Those are the rules!"

Ron lunged for the bill and in the process

sloshed the soapy water across my heart-shaped bull's-eye.

At the far end of the tent, the band kicked up with "Who Stole the Kieshka!"

I stifled the urge to scream and grabbed a napkin from the nearest Flaming Sausage waiter. While I sopped Tide off my dripping shirt, he lit his tray.

"Opa!" At the nearby tables, lunchtime drinkers all lunged sideways as the whooshing flames blasted hot air across them and across the table full of counterfeit money. The bills rippled in the heat.

Eva moved the stack of counterfeit twenties while Ron chased the feed-capped man across the tent.

"You can go now," she said.

I frowned. "Aren't you going to tell me what it means?"

"It's classified," Eva said. She turned her back again.

I stood there a second and watched Ron make his way to us with the bill. I let the Rubik's Cube twist and turn in my brain.

I stared at the agents and pointed my finger at the bill. "Do you want to know what I think?"

Eva turned around to face me. "No, I could care less what you think. *If* you think."

I leaned in close and angled myself to

block the angry citizens waiting to fill out their triplicate government forms. I poked my finger at the bill in Ron's hand.

"I think we have a big deal counterfeiter here. He made the mistake of hiring some petty crooks, the Cheerleaders. The petty crooks got greedy and stretched the ink with their tattoo parlor's ink. They were either in cahoots with Fred or they weren't. And they either are with Walter or they aren't, I don't know. And they took my . . . my old friend . . . Nancy Schnebbly. And they're framing Harpo Pentwood, the man who saved my life last night."

Eva opened her mouth, but no sound came out.

"I know this too," I said. "You guys are frying up guppies here in the Oom-Pah-Pah tent while the big bad pike chew your asses off out there." I jabbed my finger at town.

Ron and Eva and the other agents all looked at each other. I knew it was true.

"Oh, and Eva, one more thing," I said. "Just because a woman's clothes fit better than yours, doesn't mean she's stupid."

A grin twitched at the corner of Ron's mouth.

I turned on my lovely semi-law enforcement heel and marched out of the tent.

TWENTY-FOUR

I headed out to the street. Soapy water soaked through my T-shirt and dribbled into my bra. I was twenty minutes late, and I was irritable as hell. A solid line of pickups dragged empty boat trailers around the block in front of me.

An SUV pulling an empty rig rolled up beside me.

"Hey! Those yahoos in the tent just confiscated forty bucks of my money, and I'm pissed!" the driver hollered. "Plus, I've been circling the block for ten minutes. This festival sucks! Where the hell am I supposed to park this thing?"

"Do you think I care?"

Albert Schwenck's grinning face leered at me from his poster on a phone pole across the street. I represented the Elk County Sheriff's department and the people of Mudd Lake. I represented Ben Williamson.

I heaved in a breath and tried to count to ten.

The guy muttered, "It figures. Typical Mudd Lake."

He let off his brake and rolled a few inches.

"Wait, that way!" I jabbed my arm at the lot behind me. I pointed to a space next to the vacant brick building. Thanks to Wal-Mart and the mall and the bypass highway, downtown had plenty of parking, not that anybody else seemed to notice. Cars and trucks and hauling rigs were crammed willy-nilly with wheels up on the curb. Some had parked on the sidewalk, a few had managed to pull up into yards.

Within an hour, my shirt had dried, and I'd filled that lot and three more along the waterfront. I felt a little better.

I moved to the lot across from Mudd Lake Savings. They'd reopened and while I directed parking, I watched customers come and go. I had two spaces left in my current parking area when Mudd Lake's only public transportation, the little Dial-a-Ride bus, chugged to the curb. The doors wheezed open, and I stared. My heart leapt against my ribcage. A dozen Devil's Cheerleaders lumbered down the steps. They surrounded me.

"Uh-oh," I said, and hiccupped.

The Cheerleaders all stood and looked at each other for several seconds. A couple of them cleared their throats. One coughed. They looked confused.

"Snake ain't here, so you're supposed to say it, Bull," a short biker with a stringy ponytail whispered. "Go ahead. You can do it." He pointed at me.

A heavyset man stepped forward. I resisted an urge to reach out and hook my finger in the thick ring dangling from his nose. I blinked a few times. Maybe I was developing a death wish.

"Oh, yeah . . ." Bull cleared his throat and huffed up a breath. He strutted forward. "We had to take the Dial-a-Ride on account of our bikes are all smashed up." He jabbed a finger into my bull's-eye. "On account of *you!*"

I winced and backed up.

" 'Bitch,' call her a bitch," somebody hissed.

"Keep it up boss, you're doing great." A guy with a half-helmet the shape of a salad bowl shoved me back into the center of the ring.

"I ain't the boss, I'm the acting boss," Bull said. He looked at me. "The DC's follow a very strict business model these days."

"So I've heard," I said.

The Dial-a-Ride idled at the curb behind him. The doors wheezed open again, and the driver leaned out. "Are you guys going to be long? I've got a grocery run over at the Senior Center at two."

"Just a second." Bull held up a grimy finger. He patted his pockets and pulled out a crumpled index card. He frowned at it, and his lips moved while he read. He shoved the card back in his pocket and poked his face in mine. He narrowed his eyes and glared.

I tried to back up, but somebody pushed me forward.

"You bitches are dead meat. You and that old movie star and the other two." Bull poked at my bull's-eye again.

"It was an accident." I scanned the vicinity for any sign of help. I could see the agents in the tent, but I was out of earshot. I couldn't help it, I had to ask. "Are those notes?"

"Uh-huh. Just a second." Bull read some more and resumed his glare. "People who screw with our bikes, screw with our *business operations,* they end up finding pieces of 'em all over western Michigan. You know?"

"Snake'll be so proud," the guy with the

200

straggly ponytail said.

A couple of the Cheerleaders nodded at Bull.

"You're doing great," the guy with the salad bowl said.

"Take that helmet off, Skinx. We're using the frickin' Dial-a-Ride," Bull said. He poked my shoulder, and I staggered back a step. "You are going to die a slo-ow death, . . . bitch."

I lifted my chin and hoped the trembling wasn't obvious. "I'm an auxiliary deputy. You — you shouldn't threaten me."

Bull pulled out his note card again and glanced at it. He nodded to himself. "Yeah, a slow death, and then we're gonna torch this entire town."

They all made mean faces and glared at me.

I smelled him before I saw him. A faint spicy scent mixed with some primal jungle pheromone that made the hairs on my neck snap to attention. Other stuff snapped to attention, too.

"Are these men bothering you?" Jack Donner slid up beside me.

"Um . . ." I took a few steps back, out of Jack's gravitational field and hiccupped. "Kind of."

Jack had the kind of body that clothes

never seemed to disguise. The bikers ogled Jack's biceps rippling through his light-weight sports coat. Jack bounced a little on the balls of his feet and flashed a smile at the Cheerleaders — a feral smile.

Jack held a finger to his earlobe.

A memory of myself teething on that same earlobe popped into my mind. I blinked and took another step backward.

"Did I hear correctly?" Jack said. "Burn this town? My, my, my. I believe that is what, in my line of work, we call a threat to Homeland Security."

The bus doors creaked open behind Bull. The driver bent over the wheel and said, "You're making me late. Those Seniors get ornery if I'm late."

"Wait one minute, my good man." Jack shrieked out a loud whistle through his teeth.

Ben was right. He had awesome teeth.

Agents flew out of the Oom-Pah-Pah tent, guns drawn.

"We seem to have a band of terrorists right here in little Mudd Lake, people," Jack said.

His agents corralled the Cheerleaders and pointed pistols at them.

"Hey, we didn't really *do* anything," one

of the Cheerleaders said. "You can't arrest us."

"You don't have to do anything," Jack said. "You barely have to say anything. That's the beauty of Homeland Security on the new frontier." Jack turned to his agents. "I'll make a few calls. Take them to the National Security Agency's holding area out by Grand Rapids. Tell them to lose the key."

One of the bikers said, "Can you keep us there a long time?"

Skinx fiddled with his chin strap. "Yeah, that'd be a good idea. Lock us up a while, would you? Then we'd be safe from the Coach."

"Who the Hell is the Coach?" I yelled.

Both bikers and Feds ignored me.

Jack's agents commandeered the Dial-a-Ride and its driver and drove off with the gang of Cheerleaders.

Jack and I watched the little bus chug down the street. At the waterfront, crowds watched the fishing boats dotting the lake.

"That was fun," Jack said.

"Uh, thanks," I said. My knees felt wobbly. "That was great. Scary as hell, but great."

"So . . ." Jack said. "Speaking of great — great to see you." He looked me up and down, and a whisper of a smile played around his lips. "Great uniform."

I opened my mouth to speak. I hiccupped instead. "Sorry. Tacos for lunch."

Jack took a step closer and that spicy, musky scent enveloped me. His dark eyes trapped mine, and my knees grew more rubbery. "Did you by any chance miss me?"

I hiccupped at him and eased back a few more steps. "I'd love to chat, but I've got to go. I have a rehearsal. A theatre rehearsal. I'm playing a plant."

"Wait." Jack's smile disappeared. "I know you think Harpo Pentwood isn't involved. My agents told me about the tattoo parlor and what you said in the tent. You've got some of it right, but it was Harpo's car. He has the weapon and the money. I can lock him up and throw away the key." He jerked his head toward the Dial-a-Ride. "Same as those idiots."

"I think Harpo's a patsy," I said. "All those other Cheerleaders, they report to a guy named Snake. But they are all terrified of this other guy, Coach. You heard them."

"True. But I think Harpo can lead me to Snake. Snake's in this thing deep. And once I get him, I can learn the identity of the Coach." He scanned the street, came back and homed in on the bull's-eye over my breasts, then locked my eyes again. "The

Sheriff tells me you saw Snake in your alley before my agent was shot. You need to know he's dangerous, and that he may come after you."

My heart jackhammered in my chest, from fear or Jack, I couldn't tell which.

"Just watch yourself," Jack said.

Jack produced a card and slipped it in my front pants pocket. He ran his finger down the edge of the fabric and let his knuckle graze my hipbone. Electricity sizzled through me, and all my light fixtures flicked on at a thousand watts. I reminded myself that Jack was one naughty, naughty boy. My bulbs blazed brighter in response. I took another step back, hiccupped, and cursed my faulty wiring.

That whispery smile played around Jack's mouth again. He licked his lips and looked at my hips. "Damn fine uniform . . . damn fine." He let the smile show full force and slide into a grin. "You look good enough to eat."

"Hic!"

Jack gave a little salute. "I'm sure we'll see each other around town."

He turned and walked away. I was glad I'd worn black today. I was soaked with sweat.

TWENTY-FIVE

I told myself that this Snake person was long gone. He'd hung murder and mayhem and missing people and accessory to robbery all around Harpo's neck, then skipped town with his money machine. The Coach probably went with him.

But what if Jack was right? What if Snake didn't skip town? I half walked, half trotted back to the Egyptian. I tore down three Albert Schwenck posters on the way.

In front of the theatre sat a rusty, wood-paneled pickup truck. I stopped on the sidewalk at the far side of the Acadia building. Was that Snake?

The door creaked open, and a squat man chomping a tattered cigar hopped out. His door panel held a magnetic sign, "Johnny Q-Repo Man."

I kept walking toward the theatre.

"Are you the deadbeat?" he said. "I'm here to pick up the puppets."

"I am not a deadbeat." I held my palms up in the air. "Honest. Something unexpected came up. We were robbed. Besides, I'm working on getting the money right now."

"Man, can't you losers come up with a better line than that? Most of you don't work — what do you do all day? Drink? Watch soap operas and smoke dope? I've heard you theatre people like dope." He followed me between the plaster Isis and Osiris statues to the gold-painted front door. "No pussy footing around here. Joe Splotski wants his puppets. Let me in, and I'll get them."

I pulled my keys out of my purse and unlocked the door. I opened it a crack and scooted inside. I wedged my head in the door. "I was supposed to have until Monday. At least give me a couple of days."

"No can do," Johnny Q said. He pushed at the door.

I slammed it on him and twisted the lock. Sheesh.

I stalked across the lobby and yanked the throw rug over the loose floor tiles on my way. Someone from the crew had dragged the broken fountain into the coat check room and hung a *Little Shop* poster over the hole in the wall — the one with a passed-out Kitty in her pink negligee. She drooped in front of the Audrey Two's gaping jaws. Stacks of the posters sat on the counter.

At the concession stand, I snatched up the lobby phone and dialed Joe Splotski's number. I looked up at the ornate plaster ceiling. It was still water stained, but it was patched, and so was the roof above it. All this work. All this money and still so much to do.

"We need until next month, and we can pay you," I said. "Like I said, we've had a . . . series of hardships here."

"Hardships, my ass," Joe said. "You're a loser. Either pay the balance or hand the Audreys over to Johnny."

"You said we had until Monday before. And we had installments. You changed it. That's not fair," I said.

"So what?" Joe said.

"Don't expect to get our business when we're successful," I said.

"Hah! Successful!" Joe laughed so hard he triggered a coughing spasm. It sounded like he was hacking up a hairball.

I waited and reminded myself to be calm.

When he regained his composure he said, "You're funny. I'll give you that. Just to show you I've got a heart, I'll let you keep the bucket of blood."

"You're a real sport," I said. "We'll pay you next Monday, okay? I promise."

Joe Splotski was still yelling when I hung up.

I grabbed a box of Junior Mints from the concession stand and dumped half of them down my throat. With minty chocolate stuck in my molars, I stomped my way into the theatre.

In the auditorium, stage lights blazed on act one's rehearsal.

Patrice trotted over and stood beside me. We watched the stage.

"La-la-la . . . do-dooo! Somewhere that's Greeeeeeeen!"

Seymour's dentures slipped down and clacked audibly, and Kitty's voice warbled three keys away from her target.

I winced.

"Do you think they'll notice that nobody, like, really knows their lines?" Patrice fingered her eyebrow rings and watched the stage.

I patted the bouncy black rubber bracelets that covered her arm. "This is the Players. Nobody expects them to know lines."

I remembered the CracklePops Foundation.

"Almost nobody," I said.

Kitty and Seymour wound up their scene

at earsplitting decibels. Other cast members cheered.

"Oh good, Kate." Verna stepped out from the wings, "You're here."

Verna.

I made myself march down the aisle, sidestepping the hooked rug in the shape of a teddy bear that now covered our blood-stain.

"I need to talk to you," I said and grabbed Verna's elbow. We headed to the Green Room, where I told her about Harpo's arrest.

A few minutes later, Kitty appeared from the dressing room in her pink negligee costume. Her skinny thighs poked out from the pink feathery hem, and her neckline drooped to one side. She hiked it up by one shoulder.

"Is this about the case? Did you find Walter?" She slipped inside and closed the door. "We could sure use that bounty. Did you see that guy out front? No respect for the performing arts, whatsoever." Kitty looked from me to Verna. "Good Godfreys, what's happened now?"

"Oh, my stars." Verna patted her chest over and over again.

I slunk deeper on the sofa and stared at the floor.

"I can't believe they took my Harpo." Verna patted again. "My, my, my."

My stomach felt like I'd swallowed a box of carpet tacks. I filled Kitty in on what we'd found in the Taurus.

"Why, I never would have thought to check that car's license plate last night. He was so nice to us and all." Kitty patted Verna's hand. "Are you sure I can't make you a martini? Just this once?"

Verna shook her head.

"Well, don't you worry," Kitty said. "Kate's good at this kind of thing. Remember when she killed her second husband? She got herself off the hook for that, didn't she?"

I said a silent *give me strength.* "Kitty, I didn't kill my second husband, and I was only married one —"

"Details." She flapped a hand at me and kept her eyes on Verna. "And you were a *spy,* dear! Remember your government work?"

Verna straightened her shoulders. "You're right. This just won't stand. Land sakes, I can't let this stand." She grabbed her purse from the counter and tossed it over her arm. "I'm calling Charlene," Verna said. She went to the house phone and punched in Charlene's number. After a brief conversation, she marched out the stage door.

Twenty-Six

"I hope Charlene can help her." Kitty tugged at her droopy neckline. "My alterations will have to wait."

Kitty slipped into her street clothes. She told the cast Verna had had an emergency, and they'd run through the rest of the rehearsal without her.

She lit up her smile. "The show must go on, my darlings."

At the break before the final scene, I walked to the stage.

Several cast members eyed me warily.

"I hope you practiced some," Scotty Forsythe said. "At least so you don't get hurt."

"Or hurt anybody else," Seymour said. "My wife heard about you and tripled my life insurance."

Our insurance-selling sound man nodded. "Business has been good around the Players since you came on board."

I glared at him. Two crew members

wheeled the big Audrey Two into place.

"Everybody take five while Kate warms up," Kitty said.

The actor who played Mushnik, the florist, shook his head. "We should just scrap this whole shebang. We're already missing our Ronnette, and Kate's a menace to the performing arts."

He grumbled to himself and trailed the rest of the cast offstage.

"Oh, don't pay attention to him." Kitty aimed her smile at me. "You'll be stellar. Simply stellar."

I shook my head and groaned. "I'm horrible!"

Kitty waved a hand. "Details."

All I wanted to do was help Verna, and I totally sucked at the Audrey, but I was stuck, at least until Johnny Q found a way inside. Or until I found some money to pay for puppeteers, not to mention puppets.

"Patrice, I saw that the bank's open," I said. "Did they get a new manager? Can they do loans?"

"They brought in some temporary dude to run things. They don't need me until next week," Patrice said. "Which is cool, because of the show. Wait until you see what I did to your Audrey Two. Ben helped, and it went really quick."

"Ben helped with the Audrey Two?" I slapped guilt for my Jack Donner inspired wiring problem on top of the guilt mountain I already had going.

"Ben met me with the Tahoe before work, and we picked up the equipment and came over." Patrice crossed the stage to the puppet. "I'm really excited." She pointed to the Audrey Two. "Check it out."

I shoved everything else out of my mind. I hunched down and stuck my head through the fabric at the back of the puppet's noggin. "It's like — like a little spaceship!"

I slid into the secretarial chair and looked at the wiring strung over my head. I flicked a switch on the small computer monitor mounted on the chair's extended arm, and a black-and-white view of the set flickered to life.

Patrice stuck her head through the opening. "I wired an infrared camera above the stage. You can see the whole set. How cool is that?"

I nodded — speechless. Patrice had just loaded God-knew-how-much equipment into a theatre prop on the verge of repossession.

"And this." Patrice reached for the other arm of the chair and hit a button on a joystick. "You switch cameras here, and this shows you the wings."

An image of the empty stool where Scotty Forsythe sat to sing the Audrey Two's part showed on the screen.

I pumped enthusiasm into my voice. "Cool," I said.

If Johnny Q got a hold of this, we'd lose this equipment. Who knew if we'd get it back.

"Don't switch cameras when you're moving, or you'll get confused," Patrice said.

"Oh, like we need to worry about *that,*" a voice in the little knot of people offstage said. "We're worried she'll kill one of us."

"Or somebody else will! This place is a deathtrap."

I ignored it and pumped more happy sounds into my voice. "Patrice, this is great."

She beamed at me. "Get in and roll toward the Mushnik counter."

I fought back the dizzy, out-of-synch feeling. I worked my feet and rolled my chair. I watched on screen as the Audrey Two moved toward the florist shop's counter.

Patrice grinned into the camera. "Awesome."

"This is amazing, Patrice. Um . . . whose stuff is this?"

"It's on loan from some buddies of mine,"

she said. "Flip the switch by Audrey's eye-ball."

I found the switch and flipped it. The beginning bars of *Little Shop* came through.

"This plays the whole sound track from the Broadway show. The Mudd Lake Players' version sounds . . . different, but it'll give you something to practice with," she said.

I heard Kitty's voice, then watched her on my screen. She walked to center stage.

"Let's run through Kate's numbers," she said.

I got dizzy at first. I focused on the video screen. I hiccupped now and then, but somehow I managed to move the big jaws with Scotty's voice and get close enough to my marks that I didn't hurt anybody. After a few minutes, I forgot everything and watched Audrey on the screen and made her do what I thought she should do. In the final few minutes when I had to swallow Kitty, I backed up to the opening in the side curtain, rolled my chair out of the way, and stood. I used the rods to make Audrey grow taller and I pulled Kitty through the back of Audrey Two's big mouth.

Kitty climbed around me. She grinned that thousand-watt smile. "Stellar!" She scooted out the back and disappeared into the wings.

A few minutes later, I ran through the same moves with Seymour.

"Not bad," he said as he crawled past me.

While I pushed the rods up again and made the plant tall for the finale, I watched on the screen and concentrated. I moved the giant plant's head and worked her jaws.

Finally, it was over. I was drenched and exhausted.

I rolled out of the Audrey. The cast and crew all stared.

"What?" I scanned the set for fallen bodies. "What'd I do now?"

Kitty clapped her hands, and soon the rest of the cast joined her.

I swiveled to see what they were clapping at. I looked from one member to the other.

"Me?" I said. I pointed to my chest.

After the shock wore off, my heart swelled, and I took a little bow.

After the final song, people picked up their things and headed for the front doors.

Crap! Johnny Q!

I called after them. "You see a little guy smoking a cigar, just ignore him, he's a — a. He's a joke! Yeah. You know how some people, they put fifty pink flamingos in your yard? Well, Splotski's sent me this guy. Heh-heh." I fluttered my fingers. "Bye, now.

218

Funny, huh?"

Muttering came to me as they trudged toward the door.

"Just when we had a little hope."

"Here we go again."

TWENTY-SEVEN

"Kitty, lock the lobby doors after them," I said. "If that man's out there, don't let him in."

"No worries!" Kitty trotted after the cast and crew.

I ran upstairs. I changed out of my sweaty uniform and took the world's fastest shower, then punched the bank's number on my phone and convinced the new manager to see us.

I met Kitty in the lobby just as she closed the door after the last crew member. I grabbed the stack of *Little Shop* posters and shoved the big metal staple gun in my purse.

"Let's go sell this new bank manager on the value of the performing arts," I said.

"Marvelous idea." Kitty grabbed her fez from the coatroom shelf and stuck it on her head. I yanked open the door.

Johnny Q, Repo Man sat in an aluminum lawn chair on our concrete walkway. He scratched at his beer belly and swung his feet from their perch on a plastic cooler.

"You ready to pay up?" he said.

"We'll be back with money," I said.

"We will?" Kitty looked at me.

"It could happen." I patted her arm.

"Hah! Typical deadbeat answer." Johnny plunked back into his chair and produced a copy of *Hustler.* "I'll be here."

Kitty poked her finger at Johnny Q and looked at me. "Kate, can't you do something? Arrest this person and so forth? Can't you at least make him move to the alley?"

"I'm not going in that alley," Johnny Q said. "People get shot in that alley. That alley is the Alley of Death."

I totally agreed, but I wasn't telling him that. "Come on, Kitty."

I grabbed her arm. She adjusted her fez tassel, and we marched down the street. It was slow going because, on the way, I stopped to staple a *Little Shop* poster over every Albert Schwenck I saw.

Chiffon and Rhonda stood behind the bank's counter. Rhonda looked up briefly, then returned to her customer. She dipped the corner of a twenty dollar bill in a bowl of sudsy water and squinted at it.

I walked up to Chiffon's window. "How are things going after . . . everything?"

Chiffon glanced toward the blond man in Fred's old swivel chair. "It's a real mess. The guy from our correspondent bank wants triplicate copies of everything. He keeps talking about irregularities and accounting issues." She looked his way again. "And a lot of counterfeit bills slipped through for deposit here. Nobody's real happy about that either, let me tell you."

I snuck a peek at Rhonda. She'd stayed in earshot the whole time.

"Is that laundry soap?" I pointed to the sudsy bowl next to Chiffon's elbow. "That should help find the counterfeit bills, right?"

"Nah. We shouldn't need that, but the town's swimming in so many counterfeits, we're using the soap to separate the one kind from the other."

She eyed the man in the corner office again. He talked on the phone while he tapped computer keys.

"We were all set to get a loan on Monday before . . . everything happened," I said. "For the Egyptian Theatre Guild."

"Yeah, I remember," Chiffon said.

Kitty'd stayed silent while I talked to Chiffon. She was watching Rhonda. Rhonda's customer left, and Kitty crossed to her window.

"Is that the boob job Kate told me about?"

Kitty poked Rhonda in the left breast. "I've been thinking about getting one of those. I don't fill out my negligee all of a sudden, but due to time constraints with the upcoming show and whatnot, I thought I'd use socks instead." She looked down at her own breasts that roosted somewhere just above her middle. "And I heard your boobs didn't turn out too well."

Rhonda stared wide-eyed at Kitty for a second.

"Well, if you get a boob job, don't go to BYOB," Rhonda said. "They're a bunch of hacks." She reached for her top button.

I leaned over and tugged Kitty back to Chiffon's lane.

"I think we need to go in now," I said.

The manager had hung up the phone.

Kitty patted my arm. "Verna and I took a class: Connecting with Strangers, over at the Senior Center. They taught us this whole thing. You should build a bridge when doing business with a stranger. Find some common ground." Kitty smoothed her hair and adjusted her fez. "I'll handle it."

The manager motioned for us to join him.

Kitty breezed in ahead of me. "Darling!" She stuck out her hand. "I'm Kitty London. It's a pleasure to meet you, really." She sat down and crossed her legs. "We hope we didn't keep you waiting, but we needed to hang posters along the way for our upcoming show. I do believe we covered every single one of that idiot Albert Schwenck's campaign posters." She shot off a merry chuckle.

I shook the manager's hand and sat down. A single picture occupied the credenza behind him. It was mounted in one of those wooden frames with the sayings around the edges — *my dad, pops, father, dear old dad* — and the face looked familiar, very.

My heart dropped.

I scanned the bank manager's face for visible nose hairs and found them. My focus shifted to his name tag: Albert Schwenck, Jr.

I suppressed a groan.

The blond man glared at Kitty and pulled a file from his drawer. He scanned through several pages. "Let's see . . ." He made tsk-tsk noises and flipped papers. "I see so many irregularities here that we would have to start any process for a loan over from the very beginning."

He smiled and threw our file in the wastebasket.

"Hey!" I dug it out. "Don't do that!"

He snatched it from me and held it out of my reach.

"What kind of irregularities?" I narrowed my eyes at him.

He opened the folder and leafed through it. Jabbing a finger at one of the forms, he said, "Missing documentation for one thing. We need itemization of your overhead costs and your ticket sales. CPA records and . . ."

Kitty brushed a hand at him. "Don't be silly. This is the theatre. We can't be bothered with all of that nonsense —"

I cut her off. "We have records," I said. I thought about the missing benefit cash and how that would look. My heart sank. "But Fred seemed to think we didn't need —"

"It will be at least thirty days." He crossed his arms, leaned back, and smirked at us. "That is, if your credit's good."

I thought of Splotski's and Johnny Q. "We were all set before —"

"Sorry to interrupt," he stood up and snatched the phone, "but I'm supposed to call the sheriff if I see anyone matching that description." He gestured toward the big windows lining the lobby.

I turned, expecting to see Walter. Instead, I spotted a large man with a shaved head and a cobra tattoo. Snake.

I thought of Rhonda's own tattoo. Rhonda formed the curvy line that connected poor Fred Schnebbly to Snake and the Devil's

Cheerleaders.

Snake disappeared from the window, and Rhonda headed for the back door. My heart skipped a couple of beats on its way to the up escalator.

"Make that phone call to the sheriff," I said over my shoulder. "Tell him to hurry." I cut across the lobby.

TWENTY-EIGHT

"Chiffon, where does this door lead?" I jogged past her.

"The parking area," she said. "Rhonda goes out there to smoke."

Snake terrified me, but at the same time, I didn't want Rhonda — maybe our only connection between Fred and the Cheerleaders — to get away.

"Kitty, wait here," I said.

Barely breathing, I opened the door a crack and peeked through. Rhonda stood near a picnic table.

"Thank God, it's you." Rhonda lit up a Virginia Slim and blew out a plume of smoke. "I think my old boyfriend's trying to kill me."

I poked my head out and searched the area for signs of Snake. Nothing.

"Was that your old boyfriend in the window?" I said.

"Uh huh." She sucked on her cigarette.

"Snake. All week long, weird things have been happening. You know?"

I nodded. I knew.

Boy, did I know.

She hit her cigarette again. "Last night at my brother's I was unloading boxes. This stuff leaked out of my van and went all over his driveway. My brother said my brake lines had been cut."

"So, why didn't you call the cops?" I said.

"I was afraid to," she made a seesaw motion with her hand, "you know, rock the boat. My brother patched up my brakes, and I was just going to let it go. Take it as a warning, you know?"

"A warning about what?" I stepped out the door.

"Never mind." She looked away. "I should've kept my mouth shut just now, but I got scared when I saw him in the window."

I walked around to look her in the eye. "Rhonda, what was the warning about? Why would Snake try to kill you?"

"I wish I'd never introduced Fred to the Cheerleaders," she said. "Now, I think maybe I know too much."

"You introduced Fred to them? Why did Fred want to meet the Cheerleaders, to meet Snake?" I said.

"He told me he had a business proposition for them," she said. "Something about taking them to the next level, whatever that means."

I swept the area with my eyes, watching for Snake. "Fred didn't have a nickname, like Coach? Did he?"

Rhonda shook her head. "Just Fred . . . or Schnebbles."

I fought back a wince.

Ben came through the door with Kitty on his heels.

"We've searched the area," he said. "No sign of Snake."

After some coaxing, Rhonda repeated what she'd told me.

She looked at me. "I've been too scared of Snake to say a word. I would have never even opened the door when you came by, except I thought it was about the theatre. I really love *Little Shop of Horrors*."

"*Little Shop*?" Kitty cut in front of Ben. "Do you know the play?"

She nodded. "I played Ronnette in the Mudd Lake high school production. Get it? Rhonda the Ronnette."

"Good Godfreys!" Kitty patted her hands together. "This is marvelous."

Rhonda shrugged. "I forget most of the lines."

"Details." Kitty flapped a hand. "You can

be in our show! It's going to be smashing. We open Friday night."

Ben was jotting notes on Rhonda's statement when Kitty tugged his sleeve. "Ben, darling, Verna will be beside herself if she can't get Harpo released. You are going to help Verna's God-boy, aren't you? And Harpo was so nice to us when Kate blew up those Devil's Bandleaders." Kitty brushed Ben's sleeve.

Rhonda stared at me, eyes wide.

"It's a singing group," I said. "No relation."

"God-boy?" Ben looked at me.

I nodded. "Harpo is Verna's godson."

"Uh-oh," Ben said.

I nodded. "You betcha, uh-oh."

Ben promised Kitty he'd do what he could, and we left him questioning Rhonda about Snake.

The Dial-a-Ride chugged to the curb and unloaded a couple of fishermen in Elmer Fudd hats. Kitty flagged down the driver. I recognized him from earlier, except that now he wore a dazed, shell-shocked expression.

"I'm going home to wait for Verna." Kitty climbed the steps.

"I'm going to move to Canada," the driver mumbled. "Maybe even Switzerland."

The doors wheezed shut behind Kitty, and the bus puttered off.

On the way home I stapled *Little Shop* posters over six more Albert Schwencks. It didn't solve any of my problems, but it felt good.

At the Egyptian, a dome-like nylon structure now occupied the area in front of my Osiris statue. Johnny Q sat in his lawn chair, his copy of *Hustler* open on his lap, a coffee cup in his hand. I sniffed the amber liquid in his cup — beer.

"What's that?" I pointed to the tent.

"That's where I sleep," he said. "Surrender the puppets, and I go away."

"I, uh, I talked to Splotski. He said for you to leave and come back in a week," I said.

"Liar, liar pants on fire." He went back to his magazine.

I sighed. "It's not fair, Splotski changed my deal."

"Not my problem," Johnny said. He turned his magazine sideways and ogled the centerfold.

I unlocked the door and slipped around it. I poked my head out. "Can't you just leave and come back after opening night?"

"No way, Deadbeat. I got a mission to do here. Capisch?"

"No. I don't capisch. Give me a break," I said. "You can see I've got some problems."

Johnny Q swatted a hand in the air. "Eh. You deadbeat theatre people all got your problems. It's from all the dope."

I yanked the door shut and locked it.

I spent a few hours in the Audrey Two practicing with the recorded sound track. I felt pretty good about it until I thought of opening night just two nights away. The seasick queasiness I knew as stage fright rolled over me in waves.

But, Johnny Q might accomplish his mission and repossess the puppets by then. Or Snake might accomplish his mission, and I could be dead — there was always a bright side.

My cell phone rang. I rolled my chair out of the Audrey and answered it.

"Verna's quite depressed," Kitty said. "She and Charlene had no luck whatsoever with those Secret agents. They wouldn't even let Verna see Harpo. His mother's so upset, she won't come out of her basement rec-room."

"Everyone's looking for Snake," I said. "And you know Ben's doing anything he can to help."

"I told Verna that you and Charlene would meet us at the Oom-Pah-Pah tent," Kitty said. "Charlene's bringing Ernie and your bags, and Elvis-Presley Zowicki is performing. We thought it might cheer Verna up."

I groaned. "Every time I go to that tent, somebody throws something on me," I said. "I hate that tent." I paused, then blurted. "And Verna hates me!"

"No, she doesn't. She and I decided we're going to join forces and go full swing after these bad guys so we can vindicate Harpo. It'll be smashing. You'll see."

I sighed and looked up into the yawning fly-space above the stage. "I'll meet you there."

I switched out of my sweaty clothes and into low-rider jeans, my Kate Spade slides, and a white T-shirt. I slipped into my tan suede jacket and tossed my heavy purse over my shoulder. I debated between the Alley of Death and Repo Man. Repo Man won, and I cut through the theatre.

Johnny Q still sat in his lawn chair. I squeezed out the front door and locked it.

"What's that?" I pointed to the green metal Coleman stove he'd erected behind his lawn chair. A pan of something that smelled like old sneakers bubbled on the burner.

"That's dinner. Old family recipe. You think I'm leaving, Deadbeat?" Johnny Q said. "Think again. I want my puppets." He pulled a beer out of his cooler, popped the top, and dumped it in his coffee cup.

"If Splotski wants to be so-so difficult," I said, "can't you at least wait until after the opener? Please? Can't you be a little flexible?"

"Flexible, schmexible." Johnny walked to the door and wiggled the handle. "Cough up the Audreys."

I stalked down the block and headed toward the Festival. At least every Schwenck had morphed into a *Little Shop* poster; even though after several, repeated Kitties in pink-feathered chiffon negligees grew a tad unnerving.

TWENTY-NINE

In the Oom-Pah-Pah tent, Verna, Kitty, Charlene, and I sat at a front-row table bordering the grassy area. Ernie lay under my feet where he glared at the crowd, a bowl of sausage crumbles locked between his shaggy paws. We picked at the tray of charred Greek loukanika.

"I tried talking to those agents, but they'd have none of it," Verna said. "He's a good boy, my Harpo."

I heaved a sigh and took a sip of my soda. "What about you, Charlene? Did you ask Harpo if he has an alibi?"

"I didn't even get a chance to talk to him. The Secret Service has him in some sort of lockdown." She pushed sausage around on her plate. "They gave me a form to fill out and told me to come back tomorrow."

Elvis-Presley Zowicki strutted past us in his black pompadour and white jumpsuit. He sported white sunglasses with mirrored lenses, even though it was now dark outside.

The crowd in the tent went wild with applause.

"I don't believe I've ever seen an Elvis impersonator use a polka band," Kitty said. "It's quite original."

"If Snake or somebody framed Harpo, I don't see how we can help if you can't even talk to him. What about his rights?" I said.

"After that threat they made at the Dial-a-Ride, the Cheerleaders have no rights. And trainee or undercover missionary or not, Harpo's considered a Cheerleader."

"Those Devil's Cowgirls are terrorists?" Kitty twisted in her seat, so she could see Elvis better. "We foiled a terrorist operation right here? See Verna? Clearing Harpo of suspicion of murder and counterfeiting will be a piece of pie."

"Cake," Verna and I said in unison.

A capacity crowd filled the tent. People lined the area in front of the concession stands and crowded shoulder-to-shoulder at the tables.

In the grass in front of the band, Elvis gyrated his pudgy hips while the accordionist wheezed out a waltz-tempo version of "You ain't nothin' but a hound dog."

I turned to check out the Secret Service table at the back of the tent. Two agents confiscated pink-tinged and more authentic-looking twenties. A knot of crabby towns-people gesticulated and argued with the feds.

I felt an electric jolt somewhere under my low-rider waistband, and a tingle shot through me. Jack Donner stood behind the agents. He leaned over and pointed to something in their paperwork. I swiveled and aimed myself back at Elvis.

After wild whoops and applause from the crowd, the tuba blatted out the opening bars to "Blue Suede Shoes."

"You know, he's way better than I expected," Kitty said to Verna.

Verna's bifocals shone as she focused rapt attention on Elvis.

Charlene leaned toward me. "It's good she's distracted." She peered back at the agents' table. "Wow. Speaking of distractions. Is that who I think it is?"

"I don't know what you mean . . ." I wanted out of the tent before Jack spotted me and my wiring short-circuited again. "I think I'll take a walk over to the midway."

Ernie wagged his tail, but planted his front feet when I tried to pull him from his bowl of sausage. I handed Charlene his leash.

"I'll be back soon."

I crossed the grass and headed for the

237

nearest exit. Halfway there, Elvis jumped on a picnic bench and wiggled his tubby pelvis at me.

"Come on, everybody. Let's dance!" he yelled.

The crowd stampeded toward the stage. A heavy woman wearing a Bavarian dirndl skirt and ruffly apron barreled toward me. She carried a tray mounded with greasy bratwurst sandwiches. I sidestepped.

"Pardon," said a voice behind me. Icy beer soaked into my shoulder and sloshed down my back.

I whirled. "Not again."

"I'm terribly sorry, miss." A swarthy man in a Flaming Sausage jacket handed me a stack of paper napkins. His eyebrows formed one giant black caterpillar over his brown, almost-black eyes.

"I'm beginning to hate this tent!" I yelled over the noise.

He leaned forward and raised his voice. In a thick accent, he said, "The tent is so crowded, but it is good for the business. Yes?"

I tried to place him.

"You may not know me, but I recognize you. You are sitting with your aunt, the famous actress, Kitty London. You must be Kate."

He took my beer-soaked hand and kissed the knuckle. "Allow me to introduce myself, I am Bud Nicholau, the owner of the Flaming Sausage."

"Nice to meet you." I extricated my hand and kept mopping. Suede. Dry cleaning this would cost more than the sale price I'd paid for it.

People wiggled and danced in the packed aisles, making it impossible to leave. I stalked back to our table and continued to mop at my arm and back. I wondered if all the planets could have gone retrograde at the same time.

I felt a hand on my damp shoulder.

Bud Nicholau stood behind me. "Would you do me the honor of introducing me to your aunt? I have seen her movies. I am quite a fan."

Kitty and Verna were swooning over Elvis's bizarre version of "Love Me Tender." I tapped Kitty's shoulder.

"Pardon me, ladies." He gave a little bow. "I had a collision with your niece and saw the opportunity to meet the great Kitty London."

Kitty beamed and reached out her hand. "How do you do?"

Bud lifted it to his lips. "I have been a fan since *Housewives from Outer Space,*" he said. "No one has ever done justice to a spacesuit quite the way you did, madam."

"Well, thank you. I wish I filled things out the same way these days." She jerked a thumb at the poster of herself in the peignoir. "I'm considering some minor . . . adjustments in that department."

"I wouldn't change a thing." He eyed the poster. "You are a marvelous woman." Bud looked at her. "Your show opens tomorrow, no?"

Kitty nodded.

Bud cocked his head toward the poster. "And you will wear that lovely pink negligee?"

"Yes, but don't expect much from that thing."

While Bud introduced himself to Charlene and Verna, Ernie scooted out from under the table. He ran his snout over Bud's leg and growled.

Bud backed out of range just as Ernie lunged. Charlene reeled the leash in, and I picked Ernie up.

"I'm sorry, his bowl's under the table," I said. "He has food issues."

Bud reached in his pocket and dumped a pile of chips from St. Agatha's casino tent on our picnic table. "I insist you all join me at the casino tent during intermission. In the meantime," he waved a hand in the air, and a Flaming Sausage waiter appeared. "A tray of our flaming sausage for the ladies."

Kitty raised a hand. "Thanks, but I think we're sausaged-out."

The waiter looked from Kitty to Bud. "Anything else, Coach?"

My jaw dropped and I snapped it shut. While he waved the waiter away, we all exchanged wide-eyed looks.

Kitty pasted on the flirty smile that I remembered from her detective movies. "We're charmed, sir." She wiggled her fingers at him. "We'll see you in the casino tent in two shakes of a rat's whisker."

"I think it's gnat's whisker," I said after he left.

"Maybe not in this case," Charlene said.

THIRTY

We waited until Elvis's intermission, then Charlene and I took Ernie to Mama's booth. After we convinced Mama that dachshund mixes always look skinny and that he really didn't need more sausage, she settled him under her back table with a bowl of water.

Then Charlene, Verna, Kitty, and I headed to the casino tent on the other side of the midway.

"I think we should call Ben," I said.

"Nonsense, dear. You know how those silly search warrants can be." Kitty swatted the air. "They just take forever."

"Besides," Charlene said, "it won't be enough to do anything. A zillion guys are called Coach."

"We'll just spend some time with him and see if we can discover something helpful," Verna said.

"I don't know," I said. "I don't like it. I

think he's our man."

We cut around Flossie's Funnel Cakes and stood outside the big white tent.

"It could be dangerous." I looked at Kitty and Verna.

"There are four of us, and it's crowded," Charlene said. "What could happen?"

In the garishly lit casino tent, we wove through the busy tables. After scanning Caribbean Stud Poker, Texas Hold 'em, the roulette wheel, and blackjack, we spotted Bud Nicholau at the head of a jammed and boisterous craps table.

Kitty scooted up to the table on one side of Bud, Verna on the other. Kitty laid her fingers on Bud's arm and whispered something.

I watched from the other side of the table as Bud Nicholau passed the dice to Kitty.

"I don't like this, Charlene. Those two are up to something," I said. "They're making me nervous."

Chips flew as bets were laid down across the table. Kitty shook the dice and let them go. They bounced off the felt wall at the far end of the table. A shout went up, and the betters laid down more chips.

"I should go over there," I said. I took a few steps.

Charlene held my arm and pulled me

back. "Just wait and see what happens. They're fine."

The dealer said something about a new point, and Kitty threw the dice again. This time they ricocheted into the air. One plunked into a drink at the far end of the table.

"Godfreys, I wonder how often that happens?" Kitty said.

Verna slipped behind Bud.

"Uh-oh." I made another move to cross to them.

Charlene held onto my arm and winked at me. "But she was a *spy,* darling."

The dealer handed Kitty a new pair of dice. She tossed again, and they skipped across the felt, then bounced off, and hit the floor. Kitty patted Bud's hand and flashed her smile.

"I've never done this before," Kitty said.

Kitty caught my eye and winked. Husband number six, the Jaguar, had been a professional gambler.

I caught glimpses of Verna behind the Greek. Without craning across the table, I couldn't see what she was doing.

I held my breath and waited for Verna to reappear. Kitty tossed the dice. A cheer went up, and chips flew over the felt as people placed more bets.

Verna slipped into view again. She patted Bud's shoulder. "Land sakes, this is too much excitement for me." She kept patting with one hand while her other hand slipped into his pocket.

Another shout went up. A few more gamblers joined the group and added their bets to the table.

"I'll be damned," Charlene said. "Verna just put his wallet back. I think she picked his pocket."

Verna held something in her hand, a slip of paper. She shoved it in the folds of her housedress.

Kitty shook her fist, and let go of the dice. They bounced off the far wall and landed, showing a four and a three. A collective groan rose from the crowd.

"Oh my? Does that mean we've lost?" she said. She looked at Bud. "Anyway, I believe intermission is over." She leaned across him at Verna. "We don't want to miss Elvis, do we, darling?"

Kitty and Verna slipped away from the table, and Charlene and I followed them to the exit.

In between the tents, Verna pulled the paper out of her pocket and said, "What do you think Bud Nicholau was doing with Fred Schnebbly's number in his wallet?"

Kitty patted Verna's arm. "What a team we make, dear. That was marvelous. So invigorating!"

Verna smiled. "It's a start."

"I think we should let Ben handle this —" I began.

Verna cut me off. "Now, now, you needn't bother Ben. Your aunt and I are just getting warmed up."

Charlene and I looked at each other.

"Oh, lord," Charlene whispered.

We slipped back to our table in the Oom-Pah-Pah tent just before the start of the second set.

Elvis stepped into the grassy area. Around his neck hung a towel. He mopped his sweaty brow with it and tossed it into the crowd. Women squealed and scrambled around the picnic tables.

A hand touched my waist, and that jolt hit me. The spicy musky smell mingled with the stale beer of my jacket confirmed it was Jack Donner.

Charlene looked up and gave Jack the once-over, then fanned herself with her empty paper plate. "Boy howdy."

Jack leaned in close and put his mouth next to my ear. "Kate."

That tingle shot through my body, and light bulbs flashed. I slid away on the bench.

Guilt washed over me. That was Ben's tingle. Those were Ben's light bulbs.

"You need to come with me." Jack took my arm. "Something's happened at the Egyptian."

THIRTY-ONE

"What?"

His face looked grim. He made a motion with his hand.

I leaned to Charlene. "Keep an eye on Kitty and Verna. I'll be right back."

Charlene fanned her plate faster and nodded.

Jack had my arm. He pulled me through the crowd.

"Is it Ben? Is he okay?" Within seconds we were in Jack's black sedan headed for the theatre.

"Ben?" He glanced over at me. "Oh, the sheriff. He's at the scene."

"Scene," I squeaked. "What scene?" I thought of Patrice, always coming in at odd hours, doing things. Nice things. "What happened? What's going on?"

We pulled in front of the Egyptian. Flashing lights from an ambulance washed across the hood of our car. I jumped out.

Johnny Q sat on a gurney while an emergency tech bandaged half his head. "I'm going to sue! This place is dangerous." He poked his finger at me. "You should have posted a guard for my protection."

"Oh, for heaven's sake." I looked at Jack. "Is he going to be all right? What happened here?"

Johnny Q moaned. "I knew I should have stayed out of that alley."

"This happened when he tried to break into the Egyptian," Jack said.

I stared at him. "Johnny Q? I didn't think he'd stoop to that. I mean —" I turned hopeful. "Can we arrest him? Can Ben arrest him?"

"Not Johnny Q. He didn't try to break in," Jack said. "Snake did."

My breath caught in my throat.

"Some kind of a fight occurred, and," he pointed at Johnny Q, "this guy got the worst of it. Snake got away."

"This is really getting to me." I couldn't stop shivering. I rubbed at the crop of goose pimples sprouting on my arm and hiccupped.

Jack watched my face. "Are you all right?"

I stared out at the distant blackness of the lake and tried to breathe. A shaky hiccup popped out.

Jack put an arm around my shoulder and squeezed me to him.

That doggone disloyal tingle skittered through me, and I felt woozy.

"It's just that p-p-people keep getting hurt or killed at my theatre." I hiccupped into his way-too-sexy-for-my-own-good pectoral muscle. "It's — it's like we have a curse or something."

"We're looking for Snake —"

I looked up.

Ben stood at the entrance to the alley.

I scooted away from Jack.

"Uh, thanks." I hiccupped.

I swiveled to Ben. "Ben! There's this guy, I think we know who — he may be the Coach," I said.

I stood between them. Ben looked at Jack. Jack looked at Ben. If they could've shot lightning bolts out of their eyeballs, I'd have been cinders in the crossfire.

Hoo-boy.

I trotted forward. "Ben! What happened? Jack picked me up at the festival . . ." I thought about how that sounded. "I was with Kitty and those guys." I fumbled around. "Watching Elvis."

Ben slid his eyes back to me. "It seems Snake tried to pry open the fire exit. Johnny Q must've heard him and gone over to see what was going on. The two of them tangled, and this guy definitely got the worst of it. He got clubbed pretty well on the side of the head."

That hopeful feeling came back. "Is he going to the hospital? Will they keep him a few days? Maybe a month?"

I called over to the tech. "He looks awful. Really bad! You'd better take him in."

The tech rolled his eyes and kept wrapping the side of Johnny's head.

Jack walked up to us. He touched my arm. "Come on, Kate. I'll give you a ride back."

"I'll drive her to the festival when I'm done." Ben glared at Jack.

I backed up and waved my palms at them both.

"No thanks," I said, "No, both of you. Suddenly, I feel like walking."

I spun around and started away at a fast clip.

That was true. Suddenly I felt like walking. To China.

THIRTY-TWO

I took my time walking back. I was disgusted with myself. My clothing reeked of beer — again, and I had an inappropriate tingle problem. I hiccupped.

What was wrong with me? I wanted to take things further with Ben. I knew I did. So what was that tingle about? And I'd let Jack put his arm around me. And it had felt good. Really good.

Yikes.

I hiccupped again and gazed over the waist-high stone wall that separated the sidewalk from the beginnings of the park. The full moon's reflection shone like a white pathway on the patent-leather of the water. Maybe I had hormone troubles or a dietary deficiency. Maybe I needed more protein or something.

I heard a noise behind me, and a muffled voice said something unintelligible.

I turned around and stared into the face

of Bill Clinton. I gasped.

All those pent-up hormones seethed to the surface. I folded my arms and scowled at him. "You again?"

I knew it was stupid. I knew I should be terrified. I planted my feet.

He took a step forward.

I shoved my fists into my hips and stuck out my chin. "Oh for cripes sake, Snake. What the hell do you want now?"

"Iguana, bitch! You know wad iguan." He cocked his head back and tugged at the mask. "You know it's me?" He struggled to pull the rubbery politician off his face.

I held my ground. "Your head's too big for that thing, Snake. You need a mask that fits."

Snake held Bill Clinton's big rubber chin away from his head. "Let me have it!"

At the bank, I'd said almost those same words to Kitty and she'd walloped Walter with the money. I narrowed my eyes at Snake, yanked my purse off my shoulder, and swung it hard. I whacked him full-on in the ear. It connected with a surprisingly loud crack and knocked his mask sideways.

"Arrrgh! Mrrrph! Mmmph!" He grabbed for his mask with both hands.

"You're an idiot, Snake!" I gripped my

shoulder strap with two hands and swung again.

There was another crack, and he staggered off balance and went over the wall.

I bent over the low barrier and looked six feet down to the sand. "In case you hadn't noticed, I'm in a bad mood."

"Mmmwwwrrph!" He lay spread eagled on his back. He pulled the mask away from his head and said, "Call me an ambulance, please."

Then he passed out.

I opened my shoulder bag and looked inside. It all made sense. Pent-up estrogen hadn't knocked Snake halfway into next week — my staple gun had.

Headlights blasted me from both directions, and two cars screeched to a stop in front of me. Ben leapt out of his Tahoe, and Jack jumped out of the black sedan. They looked at each other, then at me.

"Are you all right?" they said in unison.

I pointed. "Snake's down there."

"He jumped over?" Ben said.

They both headed for the stone structure. Ben leaned over the wall. "Whoa."

"Is he dead?" Jack joined Ben at the barrier. They both stared down.

"Mmmrph," Snake said.

"What the hell did you do to him?" Jack said.

"I got pissed-off and whacked him with my purse," I said.

Jack turned to Ben. "Now, that's scary," Jack said.

"Tell me about it," Ben said.

I kept walking.

Thirty-Three

When I got to the tent, Elvis sat at the picnic table with Kitty, Verna, and Charlene. The King's wig had slipped back on his balding forehead, and sweat glistened on his pasty chest.

I headed for Mama's booth and retrieved my bipolar doxie-poo, then waited a few minutes until I worked up the strength to join the table.

Kitty stood and waved. "Oh, I can't wait to tell you. Elvis has agreed to perform during *Little Shop*'s intermission."

Verna nodded. "He's bringing the accordionist." She gestured to the band.

Kitty gazed up to bare light bulbs strung across the peak of the tent and smiled. "This show is really coming together, even in the midst of all this crime waving and espionage and so forth. Crackle-Pops will love it."

I plopped down on the bench and

snatched a red plastic cup. I dumped the remainder of the soda from the pitcher and tossed back a big swallow. I held the cool cup to my forehead. "That's great, Elvis."

"Elvis-Presley," Elvis said around a bite of kielbasa.

I looked from Charlene to Kitty to Verna and tried to find words for what had just happened.

"I kind of caught Snake," I said finally, "over at the park entrance. Jack and Ben are sorting things out right now."

Charlene raised an eyebrow. "I'll bet."

"Dear," Verna patted my arm. "That's wonderful. Now, maybe they'll release my Harpo."

Elvis got up to go. "Are you kidding? With the murder weapon and the funny money and the getaway car? I don't think so."

Verna stood up. She shoved her elbows out and hugged her handbag over her stomach.

"We'll see about that," she said. "We'll just see."

Kitty stood and took Verna's elbow. "Don't worry. Now that we're working together, we'll vindicate the poor boy."

I groaned and grabbed another cup. I held one over each eye and waited for the throbbing to subside.

Verna said, "Kate, we're delivering Harpo's Meals on Wheels for him tomorrow."

I took the cups away and blinked. Kitty and Verna looked at me expectantly. Charlene and Elvis, too.

"Meals on Wheels," I said. Was this guy the biker's Mother Theresa, or what? I sighed. "Okay, what time should I pick you up?"

"Ten," Kitty said.

Elvis walked with Kitty and Verna to their car.

I just couldn't face the Alley of Death or the irritable and head-achy Johnny Q. My own head throbbed enough. Plus my suitcase still awaited me in Charlene's car. We headed back to her place.

Ernie planted his hind feet in my groin and poked his nose into the cool night breeze as we rode back to the condo.

Charlene shot me a glance. "So, are things heating up with you and this Jack? Or were all those pheromones flying around the Oom-Pah-Pah tent just my imagination?"

"Imagination," I said. "I don't want to talk about it. I'm thinking I might need more protein."

Charlene looked over again and raised an eyebrow. "That bad, huh?"

THIRTY-FOUR

At the condo, I slipped into the guest room and dialed Ben.

"Jack's taking Snake out to the holding area," he said. "He wants all the Cheerleaders to sweat it out in one place for a few days."

I told Ben about Fred's number in Bud Nicholau's wallet.

"And you got this, how?" Ben said.

"You don't want to know," I told him. "But we'd better clear Harpo soon, or Jack will have to make room in the Grand Rapids slammer for Kitty and Verna."

Ben waited a beat. "Kate?"

"Uh-huh?" He'd seen Jack's arm around me. I knew he had.

Silence, then, "Stay safe, okay?"

We said good night and hung up.

The next morning Charlene and I drove to the Acadia Building next door to the Egyptian. She parked and headed upstairs

259

to her office. I hoisted my overnight bag on my shoulder and skittered with Ernie through the Alley of Death.

In front of the Egyptian I skirted the nylon dome and came face to face with a waist-high hinged sign in the middle of my walkway: KATE LONDON IS A DEADBEAT.

Ernie sniffed at the tent and lifted his leg. I made no move to pull him back.

"Good dog!" I said. "That's right. Tinkle like a boy dog."

Ernie looked up and panted, pleased with himself.

The zipper came down on the tent flap, and Johnny Q crawled out. What little of his thinning hair was visible beside his bandage looked like a rodent had nested in it.

"Hey!" He swatted at Ernie. "Cut that out."

Ernie scooted behind me. I stooped and patted Ernie's long, scruffy back.

A bandage covered most of Johnny Q's face. His one visible eye was swollen and ringed with a large purplish bruise.

"You look terrible." I straightened. "You should go home and heal up."

"Give me those puppets right now, or I'm gonna sue you for damages!" Johnny Q squawked. "This place is dangerous. You theatre people attract a criminal element."

He followed me to the door.

"Go away. Far away!" I said.

"One more day until show time." He waved a theatre ticket at me.

I swiped my hand at the ticket, and he jerked it away. "Where'd you get that?" I said.

"Where do you think? I paid for it. That's what honest citizens do," he said. "They pay for things."

"Look, I'm good on my debts. Splotski cut my time to pay short." I faded left and lunged for the ticket. "We had a deal. It's not fair."

"I'm getting in." He wiggled the ticket in the air out of my reach. "One way or the other."

I snatched the deadbeat sign and scooted past him. Ernie and I slipped through the door.

As I crossed the stage, I glanced over at the Audrey Two. I'd actually been applauded at the rehearsal. Me. I smiled.

That lasted a nanosecond, until I thought of everything else. I heaved a sigh and cut through backstage. Ernie and I trudged up the inside stairs to my apartment.

I'd just made coffee and poured myself a cup when Ernie yapped and barreled for the front door. I looked out the window and saw Jack Donner.

I stuck my head out.

"Can I come in?" he said.

"Um, now's not a good time," I said. "I need to take a shower."

Jack smiled that whisper of a smile. "You smell like you just took a shower."

"I'm going to take another one," I said.

That smile played around his eyes now. It made nice little crinkly lines at the corners. That tingly feeling started up again. Ernie stuck his nose beside my shin and sniffed the air. I didn't move.

"I came to tell you, we have Snake in Grand Rapids, but he's not talking," Jack said. "He insists he didn't kill anybody, that he's not qualified, whatever that means. I'm beginning to believe it. The guy's dumber than a bedpost."

I pushed bedpost images out of my mind. I nodded. "Thanks."

"Kate? I just wondered —" He gestured toward the choppy lake in the distance. "Am I making waves for you? For you and the sheriff?"

"Oh . . . ah — no waves," I said. "It's perfectly calm." I stuck my hand out the door and slid it sideways. "Flat as a pancake around here."

Jack grinned. "That's good. You remember

me giving you my card, don't you?"

I nodded, and remembered his knuckle on my hipbone. Big tingle on that one.

"Good. Because as far as waves go, you never know," he locked me in a deep smoky gaze, "you might get the urge for some white-water rafting." He winked and trotted down the steps.

I pulled the door shut and leaned against it. I waited for my heart to slow down, then I took my second shower in two hours. This one ice cold.

Thirty-Five

An hour later, I picked up Kitty and Verna at the Senior Center, and we took the Riviera out on the highway to the Community Outreach Building. Kitty and I stood in front of the desk while Verna signed the paperwork.

"I have Patrice getting all the good poop on Bud Nicholau for us," Kitty said. "She'll have it by dress rehearsal."

Kitty adjusted her toreador's cap. Her fifth husband, the Fiat, had been a bull fighter.

After a few minutes, the girl behind the counter shoved a stack of plastic-wrapped trays across to us. "Here you go. Meals on Wheels thanks you for your support."

In the car, Verna read off the address of the apartment building. "Harpo's mother says that he always sits with Mr. Spenser while he eats," she told us. "Otherwise, he plays with his food."

"I guess I'll take Mr. Spenser," I said.

"You two can do the rest."

"Where's Harpo?" Mr. Spenser wheeled his chair out of the doorway, and I crossed the tiny efficiency apartment.

"He's on . . . vacation," I said.

I microwaved his tray, carried it to the dinette table, and pulled off the plastic wrap.

"Harpo was gonna fix my television reception." Mr. Spenser jabbed his fork toward the TV. Mr. Spenser picked at his green beans. "Do you know anything about cable television?"

I walked over to the old TV sitting in the corner and fiddled with the cable.

"Stop! You're making it worse. It's all snowy." Mr. Spenser poked his forkful of mashed potatoes in my direction. "Harpo'll get it Monday. He comes Mondays, too."

"Oh, great," I muttered.

"Huh?" He swallowed a bite of meatloaf.

"Has Harpo been delivering to you long?" I asked.

"Just a month or so, on account of my bum leg." He pointed to a brace around his knee. "Mondays and Thursdays. He's been doing Mrs. Trottman across the hall for a long time, though. Not just meals. He takes her to the doctor and everything. He even

265

uses her car, so she can stretch out in the back."

"How nice," I said. I pictured myself shuttling around Mrs. Trottman next Monday. I stopped. "Wait a second. You said Monday, right?" I said.

"Yeppir." Mr. Spenser dumped a forkful of mashed potatoes on the table and looked at me. I cut my eyes at him and grabbed a paper towel.

"You said they used her car this past Monday?" I mopped up the potatoes. "What time was this?"

"Earl-y." Mr. Spenser flicked a green bean off the tines of his fork. It slapped the backsplash behind his kitchen sink. "Oops."

"What time?" I swiped it off with the dishcloth and came to the table. Monday was the day of the robbery and Fred's murder. "Do you remember?"

"Now, there I go. I don't want to talk about it. It's the kind of thing could get me tossed in the booby hatch." He put a finger to his lips.

"You can tell me," I said. "I won't say anything."

"Uh-uh." He flicked another bean in the air. It stuck against the lampshade above us. "No booby hatch for me."

"Seriously, I won't," I said. I left the bean

where it was.

Mr. Spenser turned an invisible key at his wrinkly lips and squinted at me.

I'd read the word 'Normal' on the label on his plastic wrap. It sure didn't refer to Mr. Spenser's personality. I took it as a sign that he had no diet restrictions.

"Hey," I said, "did you know the Sausage Festival's in full swing?"

After much negotiation, I managed to bribe Mr. Spenser with an Italian Torpedo Surprise. I caught Kitty and Verna in the hall, both carrying several trays.

"Keep delivering," I said, "I'll be right back!"

When I returned from my festival run, I stood in the doorway to Mr. Spenser's apartment and stared.

"You've been busy," I said. My eyes swept past the sink backsplash decorated with several more green beans. They landed on the mashed potato mountain in the middle of Mr. Spenser's Berber carpet. It stood over a foot high and mimicked the one in *Close Encounters of the Third Kind.*

He held a big bowl of gloppy-looking potatoes in his lap. He wheeled around the mound and plopped another spoonful onto the pile.

"I kind of got inspired," he said.

"I guess," I said.

An empty box of potato flakes lay on its side next to the sink. I sighed and shoved the foil-wrapped sandwich at him.

"Okay," I said. "Tell me about Monday." I snatched the spoon and bowl and scooped potatoes while he talked.

"Monday when Harpo left to take Mrs. Trottman to the doctor's, the president borrowed his car," he said.

"Bill Clinton?" I raised my eyebrows.

He pointed a knobby finger at me. "See. There you go. I knew you'd look at me that way. They'll throw me in the booby hatch for sure."

I asked him what time this happened, and he told me the car was gone from seven to eleven.

"Thanks," I said. "Really!"

This fit with the use of the getaway car and gave Harpo a possible alibi for the time of Fred Schnebbly's murder.

"Don't tell anybody I'm crazy," Mr. Spenser said.

"You're not! I mean, I won't." I tossed the bowl in the sink. "Have a nice day."

Out front, I told Kitty and Verna what I'd learned.

"That's outstanding," Verna said.

Kitty said, "Now that we're rolling, all we

have to do is find out who the real murderer is and track down Walter von Dickel and Nancy Schnebbly."

My heart sank as I remembered Nancy. And Walter, as big a jerk as he'd been to me — there was something desperate about his behavior.

"You don't think Snake is the real murderer?" I looked from Verna to Kitty.

"Verna and I talked about what that secret agent told you, about Snake not being qualified to kill," Kitty said. "In that Connecting with Strangers workshop we took, they said some people follow very strict business rules." She made invisible steps in the air. "Hierarchies and whatnot."

I thought about the weird terms that kept cropping up in relation to the Cheerleaders. "Maybe so," I said.

On the way back to Mudd Lake I called Ben and told him about Mrs. Trottman, the car, and Harpo's potential alibi.

"I'm in Grand Rapids with Jack and the other agents. I'll check all this out as soon as I can," Ben said. He waited a beat. "But these guys want that printing press, and the Cheerleaders are the key. Tell Verna not to expect Harpo for Sunday dinner."

We stopped behind Wal-Mart and picked up the Land Yacht, then Kitty and Verna headed back to the Senior Center to have their own lunch before dress rehearsal.

Thirty-Six

I drove to the Egyptian to meet Rhonda Wollenberg for her two-o'clock costume fitting. Cardboard signs now hung around both Isis and Osiris:

WELCOME TO DEADBEAT PALACE

"Thanks," I said to Johnny.

He sat in his lawn chair ogling his worn copy of *Hustler* through his one good eye. "No problem."

Rhonda parked her van in the Alley of Death and joined me at the front door. She'd teased her hair into a big, blond cotton-candy hive and slathered on enough greasepaint to make up the entire cast.

Johnny Q closed his magazine and gawked at Rhonda's low-cut sweater.

"Who's the babe?" He tugged at his leather vest and smoothed a tuft of thinning hair over his bandage.

"Hi there." Rhonda smiled at Johnny. "Unusual place to camp."

"Just ignore him," I said. "He's leaving soon."

I twisted the key in the lock.

"Rhonda Wollenberg." Rhonda walked over to Johnny and shook his hand. She pointed to his lap. "*Hustler,* huh? I've heard you need an agent to get your picture in that one. Anyway, nice to meet you."

Johnny grinned wide enough to pull a cheek muscle. "Holy Toledo," he whispered. He stood and smoothed more wisps of hair. "My pleasure."

I taped a paper sign on the inside glass directing everyone to the stage door. Rhonda and I cut through the lobby and entered the auditorium

"I've never been in here before." Rhonda's eyes swept the auditorium. "It's really . . ." She looked up at the peeling ceiling. ". . . trashed."

"Hey." I snuck a peek at my magic chandelier. "It's better than it was. We've been working on it for months."

"It's, um, ornate." She looked up at the balcony. "Old-school, you know? But it needs a lot of stuff, huh?"

I nodded as we climbed the steps and headed backstage.

"That guy out front's kind of cute," Rhonda said. "Is he single?"

I rolled my eyes and pulled a costume from the wardrobe rack. "Try this one on."

I handed her a black spandex number, and she slipped into one of the dressing rooms.

Charlene opened the stage door. "That little guy out front is cooking something smelly again," she said.

I pulled another costume. "He has a ticket. I have to figure a way to get him out of here for tomorrow night."

Charlene said, "Maybe you should call your federal agent buddy and have him dragged off to Grand Rapids."

"He'd never do that," I said.

Charlene raised an eyebrow.

The scary thing was, Jack probably would.

Rhonda stepped into the room. The dress fit tighter than most people's skin.

"Perfect," Charlene said. "Now, we'll find you a gown."

I headed upstairs to get ready for rehearsal. I dressed in black sweatpants, a hooded sweatshirt, and my black Puma Speedcats.

I peered down to the alley. I felt bad about sending the cast through it to get to the stage door. Plus, I had to use it again sometime. I hitched up Ernie and took him down the outside stairs.

Johnny stuck his head around the building. "Oh, it's you. I thought somebody else stopped by to try and kill me."

"Don't tempt me," I said.

He joined me in the alley.

"That Rhonda's a real looker," Johnny Q said. "She don't look like your typical theatre people to me. What's her story?"

I walked out front and pulled the deadbeat signs off Isis and Osiris. Johnny followed.

"She has her problems. Her boyfriend was murdered Monday. Her former boyfriend is the prime suspect."

"So she's single, huh?" Johnny said.

THIRTY-SEVEN

Three hours later, I rolled my chair out of the Audrey. I was sweaty and pleased with myself. The Mudd Lake Players had finished their one and only full-blown dress rehearsal with our tiny high school orchestra, lighting, and sound. Even Elvis and his accordionist had popped by to run through "Jailhouse Rock."

Rhonda faked most of her lines, but then, everybody faked in the Players. And I'd done my part and operated the big Audrey Two in the final scene without even a hitch.

Patrice flicked off the footlights and walked to the stage. She said, "You guys were awesome!"

Kitty handed me a towel. "Everyone, that was a Tony Award winning rehearsal." She slipped her negligee strap back on her shoulder. "Darn thing used to fit so well."

Verna said, "The CracklePops Foundation will love us."

The two went backstage to let the Players out the door.

"Dude," Patrice said. "I finally got something on that Flaming Sausage owner, Bud Nicholau? He's got his fingers everywhere. Remember I told you Fred Schnebbly owed somebody money?"

I nodded.

"Fifty grand. For online gambling. He owed the money to one of Bud Nicholau's companies." Patrice grinned.

I mopped my face and pulled the towel away. "Fred owed Bud Nicholau that kind of money?"

"You bet. It took a while to trace. This guy, Bud, he's got shell corporations, silent partnerships, all sorts of stuff. Some of it, I haven't figured out yet."

Kitty showed up next to us. Neither of us could speak for a few seconds.

"Whoa," Patrice said.

"What do you think?" Kitty said. "Does this look realistic?"

She'd changed into cheetah-spotted leggings and a skimpy black tube top. The top stuck out well into the double D zone. Kitty ended somewhere around B.

I hooked a finger in the tube top. "Are those socks? And whose tube top is that?"

"I think it used to be yours. I found it in

the wardrobe room." Kitty peered down at her wrinkly décolletage. "Too much?"

I sighed. "Kitty you don't need a boob job. You don't need boob socks, either. You look great just the way you are." I patted her bony shoulder.

"I don't know . . ." Kitty eyed her stuffed chest.

"Why don't you go and change? It's pretty chilly for a tube top," I said. "Then maybe we can all head to the Flaming Sausage for dinner."

Kitty brightened. "This is a crime-solving expedition, isn't it? Marvelous!"

She trotted backstage.

By dinnertime, I'd switched out of my sweats and into jeans and a black sweater. I drove to the Senior Center and met Kitty, Verna, and Patrice. We piled into the Land Yacht and headed for the Flaming Sausage.

"Look at us, we're like a whole entourage of bounty hunters," Kitty said.

"We're just following up a tiny lead," I said. I pulled in under a brightly lit Flaming Sausage sign.

Verna stared up at the sign and squinted. "I'm not sure . . . I — that's . . . Is that legal?"

Patrice followed her gaze. "Dude! That sign, it's like, a, a —"

I peered through the windshield at the sign. "I think it's supposed to be a flaming sausage," I said. "It doesn't translate well into neon."

"It sure doesn't." Kitty eyed the pink neon overhead. "It's been quite a few years since I've seen one, but that looks like a —" She wiggled a finger in the air.

"Oh, look! A parking place," I said.

A large truck lumbered past us through the lot.

"Awfully late for a delivery truck," Verna whispered.

I nodded and watched it round the corner of the restaurant. "I'd say so."

Inside the Flaming Sausage, a waiter in a black jacket and bow-tie asked if we had a reservation.

"Kind of formal for a place with a pink neon whatsy-doodle on their sign," Kitty said.

The maitre d' glowered at her. "It's a *sausage*, madam, a *flaming* sausage."

"It certainly is," Kitty said.

A waiter minced past us. Fire shot from the tray he held overhead. I recognized a plate of saganaki — the flaming cheese.

When we were seated, I said, "Order me anything they don't set on fire." I stood up.

I cut across the lobby and headed toward

the ladies' room. When the host stepped away, I slipped out the front door and trotted around the building. The night air had turned unseasonably chilly. I rubbed my arms and kept to the shadows.

I stuck my head around the corner and watched as two men loaded stacks of ouzo boxes into the big truck. I twisted that Rubik's cube again. If the Cheerleaders kept ouzo in U-Haul boxes, then what did Bud Nicholau keep in ouzo boxes? And why take them *away* from a restaurant?

I called Ben. I told him about Fred's debt to Bud Nicholau and the ouzo boxes.

"I'm still in Grand Rapids. The Trottman alibi checked out for Harpo but he's still being held as a member of the Cheerleaders. We're pushing Snake about the car theft, robbery, and murders."

"It's not enough, is it? For a warrant on this place? I know this guy Bud Nicholau is the Coach," I said. "The ouzo at the clubhouse, Fred's debt, the nickname. It all fits."

There was a pause. "Kate, you shouldn't —"

I hung up.

I headed back inside and sat down. "We should hurry —" I looked at my plate and leapt back from the table. "Oh, God!" I stared at the pile of long brown fried things.

The things were covered with tentacles. "What is this?"

"Fried octopus," Kitty said. "It's the special."

She took a bite of hers. "It's really good." She pointed with her fork. "Use the tartar sauce."

I pushed the plate away and leaned forward. "Eat fast. I want to see where that truck is headed when it leaves here." I told Kitty and Verna about the ouzo boxes.

Within minutes, we'd paid the tab, and we were back in the car. We parked at the gas station a few doors down and waited for the truck.

"They must have loaded fifty boxes," Verna said. "It makes no sense."

The semi pulled onto the street, and I eased out behind it. "It makes sense if you're smuggling."

We followed the truck along a blacktopped road. I paced it at several car lengths but kept it in sight. After about thirty minutes, we reached the town of Muskie Harbor.

Patrice dug in her backpack and produced a paper. "Bud owns a business here," she said.

We passed several blocks of shabby, mostly abandoned waterfront buildings.

"I didn't realize the economy here was so

depressed." I scanned the derelict structures looming over us.

"It's really gone to Hell in a hand grenade," Kitty said.

Windows of several of the warehouses had been boarded up. I eyed the large seedy-looking building in front of us. A sign over the door read "Loukanika International."

"Loukanika, that's it," Patrice said. "This is Bud's shipping company."

I circled the block and searched for a spot between the buildings with a view of the loading dock.

"There's no way to see," I said. "I'm getting out."

Patrice said, "I'm coming with you."

Verna struggled out of the back seat. She poked her head toward the corner. "We'll pull the car around that side street and wait."

I nodded and handed her the keys.

She looked at the Loukanika sign. "If I never see that loukanika sausage again, it'll be too soon," Verna said.

Kitty nodded. "Gave me indigestion all night."

Patrice and I cut between the ramshackle warehouses. We skirted an abandoned building next to Loukanika and peered around it. On the loading dock several men shifted ouzo boxes from the truck to the platform.

"I'd sure like to see what's in those boxes," I said. "I want to get closer."

We worked our way between Loukanika and the building next door. We peered through foggy window panes at stacks of boxes.

"All ouzo," Patrice whispered.

"Or fake money," I said.

A faint shuffling sound came from the boarded-up building behind us. A dim light burned in its basement.

I bent and peeked through the boards of a ground-level window frame. I jerked upright, clutched my chest, and staggered backward.

I leaned down and looked again.

Nancy Schnebbly stood on a chair peering up at me. She still wore her workout clothes, and she had an incredible case of bed hair, but she seemed to be all right.

"I can't reach the window," she whispered. "I'm locked in."

"Patrice." I pointed.

She hunched down and squinted through the slats. She straightened. "What happened to her head?"

"Help!" Nancy said.

The front door stood in plain sight of the street. We slipped around to the far side of the abandoned building and surveyed the boarded-up windows. I pried several planks from a vacant frame and tossed them to the ground.

Patrice boosted me through, then I leaned out, grabbed her wrists, and helped her climb in. We made our way through the large empty space and tiptoed to the basement door. I slid the bolt, opened it, and came face to face with Nancy.

It really was awful bed hair.

"Are you alone?" I whispered.

"Yes. They moved me here yesterday from someplace in the woods. They had a pillowcase over my head. I brought it up to show you. See?" She shook a flowered blue pillowcase by her fingertips. "Where are we?" She looked around. "This isn't Mudd Lake, is it? Is this Wisconsin?"

"Shhh!" I said.

I turned to Patrice. "Watch the front door," I whispered.

Patrice nodded.

I looked down the dim stairwell. "Is your uncle down there?"

"Nope, I haven't seen him since that guy in the mask kidnapped me."

I nodded. "Okay, shh."

"I don't know where my uncle is," she said. "They took him away after the guy in the Bill Clinton mask told him he had to rob the party stores. Bill Clinton said he was going to shoot me! Then he said he didn't care if he was certified or not, whatever that means. Boy, am I glad to see you. I talk when I'm nervous. Remember that? Well, I still do it. I can't help it."

"You have to be quiet!" I whispered.

"All I saw was Bill Clinton, then —"

"Shh!" I snatched the pillowcase and whispered, "One more word and I put this over your head."

Nancy nodded and followed me out of the stairwell.

"We have to go back to the window," I said to Patrice. "I don't want to risk that front door."

"What about my uncle?" Nancy whispered. "He might be here somewhere."

I gazed up the dark staircase that led to the upper floors. I thought I'd counted three more levels. God only knew what was up there. Let alone *who*.

I looked at Nancy, and it was like we were little kids again. She was always smaller, less sure of herself. She'd looked to me for what to do next.

Until the panties.

I pushed that out of my mind.

"How often will they check on you?" I

asked Nancy.

"Yesterday, the guy in the Bill Clinton mask came in every couple hours with food and stuff. Man, that place was a dump! Even worse than this. Some little shed out in the woods. You wouldn't have believed —"

I dangled the pillow case and cocked an eyebrow.

"Oh, yeah. Right. Quiet," she whispered. "I don't know the food schedule in this place. I'm new here."

Patrice kept lookout while Nancy and I worked our way through the upper floors. We ducked cobwebs and dodged rotting floorboards and moved from room to room. We heard skittering and shuffling in the walls, and once my hand brushed something that crawled, and I had to gulp down a shriek — but no Walter.

By the time we'd finished, twilight had deepened to pitch black inside the boarded-up building, and we felt our way down the stairs in darkness.

At the mouth of the staircase the meager light from the street shone through the empty window frame. I made out Patrice's thin silhouette.

"It's clear," she whispered.

Creaking came from the direction of the

front door. We all froze.

In the dimness, I watched the doorknob turn.

"Come on," I whispered. I grabbed Nancy's arm and pulled her to the window. Patrice beat us there and scrambled out.

"Jump," Patrice whispered. Nancy scooted out feet first, and dropped to the pavement. Footsteps echoed through the building as I dropped to the ground.

The three of us bounded between the warehouses and hurtled down the block toward the Land Yacht.

Behind us came slamming noises and yelling in a language I guessed to be Greek. Our feet slapped the pavement as we flew toward the car.

"Oh, my god, somebody killed them," Nancy gasped.

THIRTY-EIGHT

In the Land Yacht, Kitty and Verna were still as death. Eyes closed, heads tilted back. Their jaws gaped. My heart stopped, and I skidded to a standstill. Kitty shifted to her side and closed her mouth.

I huffed up a breath and streaked to the car. I banged my hand on the door. "Wake up, you guys," I said.

Verna jerked awake. Kitty blinked at Nancy. She punched the lock, and I wrenched the door open.

"We've got trouble," I said. Patrice, Nancy, and I scrambled into the back seat.

Verna revved the engine, and we pulled away from the curb. I looked out the vinyl back window in time to see two men I recognized from the loading dock. They watched us until we rounded the corner.

I checked behind us for several blocks until we reached the road to Mudd Lake. We hadn't been followed.

I dialed Ben. "I've got Nancy Schnebbly," I told him. I filled him in on what we'd seen. "Meet us at the Senior Center parking lot," I said.

When I dove into that back seat, I hadn't thought about what it meant to ride trapped on the hump between Patrice and a talkative, slightly smelly Nancy Schnebbly. I also hadn't thought about Verna at the wheel. Verna's highest speed clocked in somewhere under thirty-five.

An hour and five minutes later we pulled into the lot at the Senior Center and glided into the space next to Ben's Tahoe.

I handed Nancy over to Ben, and Patrice puttered away on her Moped. Verna and Kitty moved the Land Yacht to Kitty's regular space and headed inside the center.

"I've never been so glad to get out of a car in my life." I nodded toward Nancy in the front seat of Ben's SUV. "That woman can't shut up."

Ben grinned and leaned in close to kiss me.

I glanced up at the apartment building and backed up a step. At least a dozen silhouettes of old folks were planted in various apartment windows.

"We're better entertainment than *Wheel of Fortune*." I pointed out.

"These folks need to get used to me kissing my auxiliary deputy," he said.

I stepped back and held up two fingers. "Two-and-a-half weeks, then they can get used to it," I said. "You'll blow Albert Schwenck away, and you're uncontested in November."

Ben folded his arms. "This plan needs some serious rethinking."

"Nancy says Snake kidnapped her to force Walter to rob more places," I said. "My guess is the Cheerleaders had pressure from Bud, or 'Coach,' to get those pink bills out of circulation."

"Yep." Ben nodded. "That's what the agents are saying. And Jack got his warrant based on your tip," he said. "They're raiding Loukanika International and the restaurant tonight."

"Good. Great. Fabulous," I said. "Now, if we can just get Harpo released and find Walter alive — I can kick his tail into Flossie's Funnel Cakes, and the scales of justice will be balanced again."

"If you're going for balance, you'll want to get rid of that man camping and cooking smelly food in front of the Egyptian," Ben said. "I could roust him, but he may get smart and get a court order — then you can't keep him out."

"I can't anyway." I ran a hand down my face. "Somebody sold him a ticket."

"That is a problem," Ben said. "Not one I can help with."

At least with Bud on his way to the slammer and Snake behind bars, I felt safer than I had in days. I headed home to the Egyptian. After a quick check around Johnny's dark tent for more deadbeat signs, I tiptoed up the side stairs. I brought Ernie down to do his business and gazed up at the starry sky. I was so happy about Bud's impending capture, I didn't even drop my pooper-scoop bag in Johnny Q's coffee cup.

I collapsed into bed and fell instantly asleep. It felt like seconds, then my cell phone was ringing. I jammed my pillow over my head. The ringing continued. I fumbled around on my nightstand, then slid the phone under the pillow with me.

"Hello?"

It was Jack Donner.

"Are you sure you saw ouzo boxes?" he said.

I mumbled into my mattress. "What?"

"Ouzo boxes," he said. "I'm in Muskie Harbor. No ouzo boxes out here."

What he'd said hit me, and my mouth went dry. I scooted from under my pillow and switched on my bedside lamp. I sat up.

"Nothing? You've got to be kidding me. What about the restaurant?"

"Clean. No sign of Walter von Dickel, no printing presses. Not even any funny money in the cash register."

"I can't imagine how they cleared it all out so fast," I said.

"This man buys businesses and restructures them. He's very organized," Jack said. "His holdings are worldwide. He —"

"He revamps businesses?" I was wide awake now. "Is that why they call him Coach? He's a business coach, not sports?"

A pause. "It could be, yeah."

"That's where Snake's whole 'not-qualified to kill' schtick comes from. Bud Nicholau was restructuring the Cheerleaders," I said.

"Maybe." Jack's voice sounded tired. "It doesn't matter. I just dragged sixteen agents to two locations at three in the morning. We found diddly-squat. A good man died trying to nail this guy, and we just blew it. Now, he's on to us."

I swallowed hard.

"Unless Snake turns over, we have nothing connecting Bud Nicholau to anything," Jack said. A long pause, then, "My agents know we acted on your tip. I'd suggest you avoid any blue suits or gray sedans you see around town for a while."

It was three-thirty a.m., and I was awake and miserable. I shoved my feet in my slippers, grabbed a jacket, and stuffed a couple of beers in my pockets. I rooted around in the back of my closet and tugged out my lawn chair. I tucked it under my arm and marched downstairs to the Alley of Death. The raccoon chattered and hissed as I crossed near the garbage cans.

"Get in line," I muttered.

I rattled Johnny Q's tent flap. "Wake up."

I plunked myself in my lawn chair and propped my bare feet on his cooler. I popped a beer.

Johnny Q poked his head out. "Jeeze, Deadbeat, you scared the hell out of me."

"I'm depressed and I need to talk," I said. I held out the other beer.

He looked around, then at me. He crawled out and took the beer.

"You look terrible. How'd you get your hair to stick out all on one side like that?" he said.

I leaned my head back and looked at the stars dotting the clear night sky. "It's been a rough few days," I said. I took a sip of my beer.

Johnny fingered the bandage on the side of his head. "Tell me about it. Hey," he narrowed his eyes, "is this a trick to butter me up, so I'll forget about the Audreys?"

I sighed. "Nah. I needed to talk. My life is a wreck."

"Join the club. The whole world's life is a wreck," Johnny said.

"Yeah, I guess," I said. "But I screwed up something really important tonight. And then there's this puppet thing." I poked my beer can at him. "You snatch those puppets before the show, you're doing me a favor. I'm going to suck. I'm terrified of the audience. Plus, I think my hormones are wacky."

Johnny eyed me warily. "If you're gonna bring up female troubles, I'm going back in my tent."

"Nah, it's just —" I stared into the top of my beer can. "Everybody thinks I'm a loser."

"Eh, Deadbeat, don't be so hard on yourself. You're going through a bad patch is all. Take me," Johnny said. "I see a nice girl like that Rhonda, she won't give me the time of day. My girlfriend's a magazine." He raised his hand and wiggled his fingers. "And —"

"I get the point." I grimaced, then slugged some beer. "Rhonda thinks you're cute," I said.

"Really?" Johnny's one visible eye blinked at me, and he straightened up in his chair.

"She does?"

"She likes you — she asked if you were single." I took another sip. "Just because my life's a mess, doesn't mean you two shouldn't get together."

"Wow. Thanks." Johnny smiled a gap-toothed grin at me. "But just so you know, I'm still taking the puppets."

I sighed. I finished my beer and went back upstairs.

I tossed and turned the rest of the night. I dreamt of the Audrey Two chasing me around the stage while Harpo and the cast from my fourth-grade nativity play cheered her on. The next morning I awoke to Ben at my door. He held out a white paper bag from Muffin Mania.

"Don't try to cheer me up," I said. "I want to stay miserable." I turned to head inside.

Ben stayed on the landing. "I'm meeting Jack. We're going over my cases and his for new angles on this Bud Nicholau thing. Unless we find something to connect him to the Cheerleaders, he'll walk."

I came back to the door and leaned against it.

Ben eyed my cowgirl pajamas. "I am this close to trashing that plan and holding a rodeo in your sleepwear."

My heart sped up, then I smiled. "You're

trying to distract me," I said. "You did a pretty good job, too, but I'm still miserable, and you're still dealing with Albert Schwenck."

"We're talking about this later." Ben fingered one of my curls. He headed down the steps. "Break a leg tonight," he called as he climbed into the Tahoe.

I gasped, and my eyes went wide. I hiccupped.

THIRTY-NINE

By late afternoon, backstage hummed with activity. Crew members scurried around and made adjustments. The cast had slipped into costumes. Some already wore stage makeup. I stood in the dressing room and zipped Rhonda into her spandex.

"You really think he likes me?" Rhonda said. "because I'm a sucker for a little guy like that."

"Yep, he's got it bad," I said.

"And a guy with an injury, well that just makes me go all Florence Nightingown."

"He likes you," I said.

"You're sure he's not married? I'm swearing off married guys."

"He's single," I said.

She smiled over her shoulder at me, and it was a pretty smile. "I'm going to go talk to him. Do I have time?"

I looked at my watch and stifled a shrieking fit. "We open the doors in an hour."

Rhonda slid into her stilettos and trotted out front.

I'd only looked at my watch for effect. My stage fright bubbled inside me like a molten witch's brew, and I'd been counting seconds, minutes, and hours like a death row inmate all day.

I peeked at my wrist again. I watched the second hand sweep around in a circle.

Fifty-nine minutes until the house opened, another hour to show time. The Crackle-Pops committee might be on the road already. Other people would be here soon.

People. As in audience.

"No worries, no worries," I whispered under my breath.

My legs felt shaky and dizziness washed over me. I sucked in a deep breath and blew it out. I watched Charlene pat powder on Seymour's jowls.

"Break a leg, darling," Kitty said. She sidled past me in the crowded hall.

I tried to smile and twitched instead.

"Just make sure it isn't my leg," Seymour muttered.

Cast and crew giggled and nudged each other.

Cripes. How could they be enjoying this? A crowd was gathering to watch us. A fate worse than death was barreling at us like a freight train. *An audience.* Weren't they terrified, too?

I hiccupped and tried another breath. I shut my eyes.

I opened them to see Ben weaving through the crowded hallway.

"We spent the whole day trying to nail Bud," he said. "It's like peeling an onion. Every business leads to another business, fake names, silent partners, dummy corporations. We found nothing concrete."

I tried to talk, but hiccupped instead. I fiddled with the strings on my black hoodie and nodded.

He bent close and studied my face. "Jeeze! You're terrified," he said.

I nodded some more. I glanced at my watch again. Forty minutes until doors. One-hour-forty until curtain.

Sweat dribbled down my forehead. "I don't think I can do this," I said. My vocal chords felt like rubber bands.

Ben put a hand on my shoulder. "Try to relax."

I swiveled my head and scanned all those calm, happy people in the hall. I grabbed Ben's arm and tugged him close. "Listen! I've changed my mind. Tell Johnny Q to come get the puppets," I whispered. I clutched at his wrist and peered into his eyes. "He's coming, right? You didn't arrest him or anything, did you?"

Ben put both hands on my waist. "Shhh, calm down."

"I don't want to be a puppeteer!" I wailed.

Silence. The cast all looked at me.

"She'll be fine," Ben said.

He yanked me into the prop room.

Ben put his hands on my shaking shoulders and pushed. He stared into my eyes. "You're going to be okay. Try counting. Come on. One — two —"

I hiccupped, sucked in a breath, and shut my eyes. I got to three. Counting made me think of sheep. Sheep made me think of the nativity play. The nativity play made me think of — My eyes popped open, and my heart raced. "I'm going to mess this up!" I moaned. "I'm going to have an attack — a seizure or something." I hiccupped. "Save me. Get Johnny Q. He needs those puppets! Tell everybody to go home."

Ben kicked the prop room door closed behind him and wrapped his arms around me. "You're going to be great," he whispered. "Truth is, I was thinking of arresting Johnny Q for illegal camping, but his tent's zipped up, and he's not around."

I buried my face in Ben's chest and groaned.

"Shhh. Patrice and I built you a space-ship," he whispered. He stroked my hair. "It's magic, just like your chandelier."

I pressed my head into Ben's chest and tried to collect my thoughts. In the middle of all this chaos, Ben had come here in the early morning hours with Patrice. He'd wired the Audrey and done what he could to help me. I lifted my head and gazed into the crystal blue infinity of Ben's eyes. Something shifted inside of me.

This man knew my secrets. He knew my scars.

I drove this man crazy, but he loved me anyway.

He loved me anyway.

I buried my fingers in Ben's thick hair and kissed him full on the mouth. Ben held me tight until both our hearts slowed down. He opened the door. "Magic spaceship," he said. He winked at me. "See you after the show."

I smiled. "Count on it."

FORTY

Minutes flew and soon Charlene was smearing my face with black greasepaint.

"The CracklePops Foundation has the whole front row center," she said.

"Don't tell me that," I said. "Do not say anything about . . . about . . . p-p-people."

She eyed me and slapped more black cream on my face. "OK then, no people. It's empty out there. Quite cavernous. Vacant. What a shame." She gave my makeup a final pat.

I got up and paced the hall. I worked my way into the wings. I heard murmuring on the other side of the heavy blue velvet curtain. Verna had warned me not to peek out. I stared at the heavy material.

The orchestra kicked into the opening strains of the overture. I hiccupped.

Just one little peek. I pressed my eyeball up to a split in the leg curtains. People occupied every seat. They talked to each other like they expected something. Something good.

Oh God.

Sweat rolled down the back of my neck. I kept my eye pressed to the gap in the fabric. I recognized the CracklePops committee from their pictures in the brochure. Behind them sat Albert Schwenck in a "Vote for Albert" hat. Sheesh.

I scanned the crowd. There was Ben, and Nancy Schnebbly, and, oh jeeze, Jack.

Did everybody in the world need to come and watch me fail?

Then I spotted a swarthy man. A familiar bushy unibrow crept across his forehead. I narrowed my eyes. Bud Nicholau.

"We're going to get you," I whispered.

I pulled my head away, and my heart kicked up speed. A killer in the audience. It doesn't get any better than that.

Rhonda stood behind me. She patted at her disheveled hair.

I raised an eyebrow. "What happened to you? Did you find Johnny Q?" A desperate glimmer that I'd get out of this flickered in my mind.

She nodded. "He's very nice. We got to discussing medical problems," Rhonda said. "He's sleeping, now." She turned pink and smoothed at her dress.

"Makeup!" I said to Charlene.

Charlene scurried to reassemble Rhonda.

Kitty and the other actors slid past me to go on stage, and Verna herded me into the greenroom.

Things were going too fast. I heard noises and people and clapping and all the things I'd avoided since I was nine. Maybe this was a nightmare. I pinched myself. Nothing. My heart felt like a bag of Mexican jumping beans on a hot stove.

"It's going swimmingly." Kitty came in and poured a glass of water. She wore her first act costume. My glance bounced to her leopard sweater.

"You look more . . . filled-out than usual," I said.

"Hmmm." Kitty looked down. "Must be all the excitement."

Other cast members dribbled in.

Out front, the accordionist squeezed out the opening notes of "Blue Hawaii" and Elvis-Presley Zowicki crooned to the audience.

"Oh my God, it's intermission already?" I hiccupped. With a trembling hand, I mopped sweat mixed with black greasepaint from my face.

"Uh-oh." Kitty lifted her hand in front of her solar plexus and sucked in a long breath. "Bre-eathe," she said. "Just bre-eathe."

I sucked up a breath. Two or three hiccups rode in with it.

The crowd whooped and hollered when Elvis finished.

Kitty patted my shoulder. "Keep breathing, Kiddo. I'm back on."

I only had one scene, the very last. *How bad could it be?* That's what I'd said.

Idiot, I told myself. *This* bad. *This* is how bad it can be. My heart punched against my ribs.

And I volunteered. After this, I was seeing a doctor about having my tongue removed.

Kitty'd left the door open. I could hear everything. I paced the greenroom like a caged animal.

Charlene poked her head in.

"They're ready for you," she said.

"Oh God! I can't do this!" The panic rolled over me.

She grabbed my hand and pulled me out of the greenroom. "Yes, you can."

"Magic spaceship," I mumbled. I climbed inside the Audrey.

Two crew members rolled me into place on the darkened stage. I hiccupped. My hand shook as I flicked my monitor switch.

Breathe. I siphoned up another breath.

"La-la-loo-loo sleepytime!"

I watched Kitty swing her hands in the air. Feathers flew off her negligee and flitted to the stage.

She crossed in front of me. My heart rammed against my chest. I was supposed to open the jaws and keep up with the singing! I bent Audrey forward and yanked the levers. I rocked slightly. I'd pulled too hard and bumped Kitty in the chest.

Crap.

On my screen I watched two argyle socks pop out of Kitty's negligee. Something clattered to the boards with them. Kitty's eyes widened.

"Ooooh, Seymour!" Kitty hugged her chest, moaned, and swooned over the socks. She lay still on the stage.

Seymour came through the door of the set, while Scotty sang, "Fee-eed me."

I was supposed to be moving my Audrey's lips again. I grabbed for the bars. My hands were slick with sweat. They slipped off.

Oh God, oh god.

"Fee-eed me," louder now.

I jerked forward and bumped the joystick. The camera flipped to a view of the wings. I couldn't see the stage.

Crap again!

Sweat dribbled down my face.

Then I froze.

I stared at my monitor. Bud Nicholau stood behind Scotty. He squinted at something on the stage floor. He shoved Scotty out of the way and ducked low. He scooted across the boards to Kitty.

No time to get out. I hit the joystick and flipped the monitor to the stage view. On screen I watched as Bud felt around the floor. Puzzle pieces snapped into place in my head. Bud saw the negligee on our poster that night. He asked Kitty if she'd be wearing it in the show. The negligee hadn't fit right since Kitty'd taken it from Walter's. And Snake and the others had been after something. I'd always assumed it was the Post-It with the serial numbers. I'd assumed wrong.

I hoisted my flower pot around my knees, shoved my secretarial chair, and lifted my feet high. On my monitor, I watched Audrey sail across the stage.

I spotted someone new on my screen. Behind me, Johnny Q scrambled toward Audrey and snatched at one of her trailing roots.

"Hey, Deadbeat!"

I heard mumbling from the audience. "That's not in the script."

Bud was on his knees. He ran his hands frantically over the boards. I peered at my screen. I watched his fingers close around a small plastic bar — a data stick for the computer. Patrice had one just like it. All at once I knew, whatever information was on that thing, it could take Bud Nicholau down. Why else would Bud risk this kind of move?

I scooted my flowerpot after him.

Bud got to his feet and moved toward the wings. Johnny Q stood in his way.

"I want that puppet, Deadbeat!" Johnny Q hollered. He tried to skirt around Bud Nicholau.

"Fee-eed me!" roared Scotty. I moved in close.

Bud Nicholau lurched forward and grabbed for Johnny Q. "You! You come with me!" He latched onto Johnny's arm.

Johnny jerked away, but Bud held fast.

I dropped my planter and lunged out of my chair. I shoved the rods out as far as they could go and grew Audrey to her full seven feet. I yanked the jaw-bars and tipped forward.

Bud turned and looked up. His mouth fell open. Johnny wrenched free from his grasp.

Audrey crashed down and dropped her gaping maw over Bud Nicholau's head and arms. I let go, and the jaws snapped shut. Bud's head poked through where Audrey's tonsils would be, his face inches from mine. Angry Greek mixed with English. Spittle flew from his mouth.

I pulled my head back and grabbed his shoulders.

Bud Nicholau struggled to slip out, but Audrey's jaws had locked around his body.

"This ridiculous town!" he thundered. "I should never have come here. Your stupid bikers! They stole from me!" He jerked his head. "Let me go!"

I gripped his neck and stood up. "Jeeze! Don't spit!" I pulled my face away. "Help!"

Scuffling sounds from the stage. My monitor was black. I heard Ben's voice.

"I've got him cuffed, Kate. Let go," Ben said.

I pried my fingers from Bud's neck and held the bars down to open Audrey's mouth. Bud's face receded through the mesh.

I became aware of cheering. I climbed out of my chair and poked my head out.

Ben held Bud Nicholau by the arm. Johnny Q, Elvis, and Jack all stood on stage. Ben handed the data stick to Elvis.

I scrambled the rest of the way out of Audrey. I was gasping for breath and drenched with sweat. My knees wobbled, and I hiccupped.

Ben locked his eyes on mine.

"Hold this," Ben said. He pushed Bud Nicholau at Jack and stepped in close to me.

His arms slid around my back. "Kate."

I glanced sideways at the cheering crowd. I nodded toward the "Vote for Albert" hat in the second row. "Albert Schwenck's out there —"

"*Screw* Albert Schwenck!" Ben growled. He drew me to him and kissed me hard.

The crowd was still clapping, and we were still kissing when the curtain came down.

FORTY-ONE

In the greenroom, Jack had the memory stick plugged into Patrice's laptop while out front Elvis belted a wheezy encore of "Don't Be Cruel."

"The state troopers are taking Bud Nicholau to jail," Ben said. "It'll take a while to figure out all the charges."

Jack scrolled through the screens. "Fred must have taken this memory stick from Bud and hidden it in the negligee. From what I see here, I'd guess Fred was about to turn evidence."

"So that's why the pony-tailed — I mean, your agent, was at Walter's apartment," I said.

"When Fred didn't show at the bank, he must've gone there looking for him." Jack nodded.

Ben looked over Jack's shoulder. "No wonder Bud was desperate for this. The data here gives us the Cheerleader's business plan and ties them directly to Bud."

Jack pointed. "Here's names, dates, and drops for the counterfeit money — shipping locations. And warehouse sites — all owned through Bud Nicholau's shill corporations." He chuckled. "And freighter schedules, delivery dates. Get this," he turned to Ben, "a ship tied to Bud's organization left last night from Muskie Harbor. We have the coast guard boarding it right now."

The door swung open, and Kitty came in, followed by Elvis. Elvis stuck his head in the fridge and rooted around.

"This negligee fits a lot better with that thing-a-ma-bob gone." Kitty fluffed at her feathery chest.

Verna pushed through the door. "He's coming." Her bifocals shone, and her voice was hushed with excitement. She poked her head out to the hall, then turned to us. "The CracklePops representative is on his way."

Kitty, Verna, and I stood close to each other and exchanged glances.

A small dark-haired man with a goatee entered the room and approached us. "Very nice show . . . unusual, although the ending, even off script like that, felt a bit clichéd."

Ben narrowed his eyes at him. "It was an excellent ending."

He looked at me. I cocked an eyebrow at Ben and nodded. "I thought so."

Kitty, Verna, and I all watched the little man from the Foundation. None of us breathed.

"Well, then." He shook my hand. "Thanks for the tickets."

He cleared his throat and turned his back on us. He pumped Elvis's hand up and down. "You're quite something, sir. The CracklePops people are very impressed."

"Huh?" Elvis popped the top on his soda.

"We would love to fund a project for you," he said.

We all looked at each other.

"You!" I poked the CracklePops person in the back of the shoulder. "What about *us*? You were supposed to be watching *us*."

He swiveled around. "Uh . . ." He cleared his throat again and shifted his weight. "Like I said, you're certainly unusual. But . . . I'm afraid you're not CracklePops caliber."

I looked at the water-stained ceiling. "Unbelievable."

Verna shook her head.

"It figures." Kitty sighed.

Jack touched his ear piece. "We just found Walter von Dickel and fifty or so ouzo boxes filled with counterfeit money on that freighter. The good stuff. It looks like they were planning to throw Walter overboard."

"I'm glad they found him okay," Kitty said. "I would have liked to have apprehended him myself, though." She jabbed a finger at the CracklePops representative. He droned to Elvis about opening his own performance center. "We could have used that bounty."

"Is he apprehended — or rescued?" I asked. "I mean, did anyone ask why he robbed the bank?" I rubbed my still achy jaw. Black makeup smeared my palm. "Or why he hit me? Twice?"

Jack clicked off his earpiece. "Here's what we know. The Cheerleaders kidnapped Fred Schnebbly. From the data in front of me, I'm guessing Fred was supposed to be in on it at first — to get Walter to rob the bank and other places. There's even a list. The plan was to get those pink bills out of circulation before anyone spotted them."

"And folks would just chalk it off to Walter being crazy," I said. "Rhonda introduced Fred to the Cheerleaders, and Fred set them up to run Bud's counterfeiting operation. Fred must have gotten in deeper trouble with Bud when the Cheerleaders tried to scam things. They stretched Bud's ink to print their own bills behind his back, right?"

Jack caught my eye and nodded. "Very good."

Ben pointed to the memory stick. "And Bud must have found out about the missing data stick, and Fred's plan to turn evidence."

"And whacked him for it," Jack said, "then he got rid of my agent."

"So why'd Walter keep stealing after Fred got killed?" I asked. "Was he afraid they'd kill him, too?"

Jack shook his head. "Walter told the Coast Guard debriefer that he didn't know about Fred's death until he heard them dedicate a song to the *late* Fred Schnebbly."

"At the Oom-Pah-Pah tent — 'In Heaven They Have No Beer!' " I said.

"That's when Walter shoved the twenty at you. Snake was nearby," Jack said. "He didn't know what Snake might do, so he hit you and ran."

Ben said, "Okay. And with Fred dead, Snake and his gang couldn't control Walter."

Jack nodded. "That's when they took Nancy. They were still doing damage control on that pink money."

The final Rubik's cube squares clicked in

place. "That's why Walter ran at the club-house," I said. "He was afraid they'd kill Nancy if he escaped."

"Yep," Jack said. "It fits."

I wrinkled my brow. "What about the Post-It in my Stuart Weitzman?"

Jack shrugged. "Fred probably kept that list to spot the bad bills at the bank. Maybe he stuck it in your boot to hedge his bets — to leave a message that could help Walter in case something happened to him."

Verna said, "And my Harpo?"

Jack pulled the data stick out of Patrice's machine and folded the lid. "His alibi's good, and the business plan shows Harpo was on the outside of the operation."

Kitty smiled and squeezed Verna's hand.

"Nancy might still be in the theatre," I said. "We should tell her about Walter."

In the lobby, I scanned the people for Nancy's gawky figure, then pushed through the doors to the sidewalk.

Johnny Q was loading a duffel bag.

"Goodbye, Deadbeat." He pulled at a tent pole. "I guess I'm moving on. It's too dangerous for me here."

I cocked my head and met his one good eye. "Too dangerous, huh?"

He gave me a gap-toothed grin and jerked his head at his truck. Rhonda wiggled her fingers at me from the cab.

"I borrowed a nurse's uniform from wardrobe," she said. "I hope that's okay."

Johnny leaned in and patted his head. "She likes my bandages."

I waved to Rhonda. "Be back for the show tomorrow."

I thought about the show and didn't even hiccup. Maybe my stage fright was gone.

"Call Splotski," Johnny said. "I put in a good word for you." He stuffed the tent under his arm and headed for his truck.

I spotted Nancy coming out the lobby doors. I touched her arm.

"Acting and everything, Kate," Nancy said. "Wow, I want to be like you when I grow up."

"Nance, you're thirty-four," I said.

"Oh. Yeah."

She followed me to the greenroom, and Jack told her about Walter.

"He almost made it to Wisconsin, huh?" Nancy sighed and got a faraway look. "I'll go there someday." She produced a checkbook. "I'm good on my word, Kate. You guys get the bounty."

"Bounty?" Kitty poked her head up. "We got the bounty?"

Nancy nodded. "You found a way to save my uncle. And me. Besides," she patted my shoulder, "I get to hang out with my friend Kate again."

Oh boy.

"I knew we'd do it!" Kitty flashed that thousand-watt smile at me. "Kate, we got the bounty!"

I smiled back at her.

And I got something else. I caught Ben's eye, and he winked. My engine gave a happy purr, and I felt something good. Something real. Something that could last.

Then Jack looked over at me. He smiled.

I waited. No jolt. No electricity. I didn't even feel a tingle.

Well, maybe just a little one.

ABOUT THE AUTHOR

Susan Goodwill has been involved in many aspects of community theatre from popping popcorn to wielding power tools. She's ushered guests, swept the stage, even taken out the trash. In fact, she's done just about anything possible for a theatre person with stage fright.

Prior to a successful career selling telecommunications, she created stage clothes for rock bands, among them Electric Light Orchestra and Bob Seger and the Silver Bullet Band.

She is a graduate of the prestigious Writers Retreat Workshop and a member of Sisters in Crime, Mystery Writers of America, American Mensa, and Jenny Crusie's Cherries.

Susan lives in a 1927 cottage-style home on a small lake in Michigan with her human and rescued-dog family.